James Adams

Burns's Chloris - A Remniscence

James Adams

Burns's Chloris - A Remniscence

ISBN/EAN: 9783744714778

Printed in Europe, USA, Canada, Australia, Japan

Cover: Foto ©Andreas Hilbeck / pixelio.de

More available books at **www.hansebooks.com**

Burns's "Chloris"

A Reminiscence

BY

JAMES ADAMS, M.D.

With Facsimile of Poem "The Song of Death"
In the Poet's Handwriting

GLASGOW

MORISON BROTHERS

99 Buchanan Street

1893

PREFACE.

It has gratified me that my little contribution to "Burns Literature" in the *Glasgow Herald* has given pleasure to many individuals. The present reproduction* (with my authorisation) will be more suitable for preservation, and after reference, than the perishable columns of a daily newspaper. When I began to pen my Reminiscence, I found material so crowd upon me, that the two or three columns I contemplated would be insufficient. In like manner, when correcting the proof sheets of this reprint, I recognised the need of amplifying and corroborating, in an Appendix, various incidental references and comments in the text, besides giving, in full, the words of the songs associated with the heroine.

I have endeavoured to emphasise the reasons that make "*a people's edition*" of Burns's writings a *desideratum* — an edition from which the head of a family can "wale a portion wi' judicious care," and read aloud in the home circle; and which can be left accessible to its sons and daughters. I indulge the hope that when such an edition is produced—as it assuredly will—a copy will be found in the dwelling of every respectable Scottish household. With this hope I have dwelt more fully in the Appendix on considerations which should influence *true*, as well as professing admirers, — individuals who *really respect* Burns,—in denouncing, openly and persistently, the unceasing reproduction and dissemination of those writings which he so lamented, repented, and would have blotted out—that he so yearningly desired should be buried in oblivion.

With these foremost inducements to publish my Reminiscence, there has been a long-existing desire to scatter the garbage of detraction spread over Chloris by Allan Cunningham, and kept preserved by the small fry of Editorial Godfathers of Booksellers' "pot-boilers," who have fed on the foul imaginations of their great prototype—*vile pecus imitatorum*, parasitic vermin crawling on the carcass of genius. I have received assurances from many intelligent correspondents, that my effort has already borne conclusive fruits.

In deprecation of criticism that may befall, it is expedient I should explain that my exercise in writing has been restricted to dry professional and scientific monographs, ephemeral communications, and discussions in newspapers on topics of public interest at the moment. And the present work has been to wile the tedium of hours that are apt to flit with leaden wings during

" the seventies and eighties of life," with one who is well conscious he has passed the time for becoming mental effort, and is lagging superfluous on the stage, but who, through life-long habits of work, must find fitting congenial occupation— possibly useful—likely to please immediate friends, and, as he hopes, gratify some of his fellow-citizens.

JAMES ADAMS, M.D.

5 WOODSIDE CRESCENT,
GLASGOW, 3rd August 1893.

The Publishers have made a pleasing contribution to my Reminiscence, in a facsimile of Burns's handwriting of "The Song of Death,"—of which I have said so much, because of its intrinsic merit, and specially because of its interest in my eyes, from its being passed direct into my hands from the hands of Chloris sixty-four years ago. I recognise this as an admirable and truly perfect facsimile, and Chloris's docket on the back adds interest to the relic. It is the work of Messrs M'Farlane & Erskine, Lithographers, Edinburgh, whose facsimiles of important Scottish documents have been much admired by competent critics of this class of artistic reproductions.

J. A.

CONTENTS.

PART I.

BURNS'S "CHLORIS"

A REMINISCENCE.

PART I.

CHLORIS, HER STORY AND RELATIONS WITH BURNS.

"CHLORIS"—why so-called? The Chloris of classical antiquity was the "Goddess of Flowers," identical with Flora, the Roman goddess. She was also the wife of Zephyrus, the personification of the west wind. But the Scottish Chloris of the eighteenth century, the Chloris from whose inspiration Burns derived, more than from any other source, many of his best songs, is the Chloris whose reality I desire to make better known than she is to many of the readers and students of the poet. For of the three pre-eminent goddesses of his lyrics—Jean Armour,

B

Highland Mary, and Chloris—although the first
is sufficiently familiar to our conceptions, and
while the second is surrounded by a somewhat
misty halo, very much due to the poet's own
devising, and the latter is rather obscured by
some ill-considered allusions of one or two of
Burns's editors and critics, *all three*, more or less,
have been the subjects of detraction. Yet I may
say, *in initialibus*, that certain of these vilifying
commentators, in common with other iconoclasts,
have erred more through ignorance or misinformation than from intention.

Of Chloris, the poetical divinity of Burns, the
Jean Lorimer of prosaic life, he says—in a letter
to Thomson, the compiler of a *Select Collection of
Scottish Songs* :—

"She is one of the finest women in Scotland ; and, in
fact (*entre nous*), is in a manner to me what Sterne's Eliza
was to him—a mistress, or friend, or what you will, in the
guileless simplicity of Platonic love. (Now don't put any
of your squinting constructions on this, or have any clish-
maclavers about it, among our acquaintances.) I assure
you that to my lovely friend you are indebted for many
of your best songs of mine. . . . Whenever I want to
be more than ordinary in song—to be in some degree
equal to the genius of your diviner airs—do you imagine
I fast and pray for the celestial emanation? *Tout au
contraire.* I have a glorious recipe ; the very one that
for his own use was invented by the Divinity of Healing

and Poesy, when erst he piped to the flocks of Admetus, I put myself in the regimen of admiring a fine woman ; and in proportion to the adorability of her charms, in proportion you are delighted with my verses. The lightning of her eye is the godhead of Parnassus, and the witchery of her smile the divinity of Helicon!"

So much by way of premise to my personal reminiscence of Chloris, or Jean Lorimer.

As nearly as I can recollect—and my memory is good—aided by collateral data, it is now about sixty-four years since I saw and held converse with Jean Lorimer—*Mrs* Lorimer, as she was designated, but probably more familiarly known to readers of Burns under the fanciful names of Chloris, or "The Lassie wi' the Lint-white Locks," given to her in about thirty of his best *and purest* poems. Mrs Lorimer was a patient of my father, Dr Alexander Maxwell Adams, long of St Patrick Square, Edinburgh. I was then at school in Nicolson Square, which is situated almost immediately opposite to the site of the Surgeons' Hall. Nicolson Square, which I am informed is a locality much changed since my day, was about a quarter of a mile distant from my home, and Mrs Lorimer resided within about thirty yards of the school, in "Middleton's Entry," a wide pend or archway through the building that formed the west side of Nicolson Square, and through which "entry" access was given to the Potterrow. Her house was one stair up, in a common staircase on the left side of the "entry" as it led from the square. I was instructed by my father on a Saturday to call immediately after leaving school—the hours of which were short on Saturdays—for a packet of papers, and to be careful in fetching it home.

The "land" or tenement was of four or five stories, and made up of numerous small houses entered by "the common stair." I was admitted by Mrs Lorimer herself, and I saw no sign of other inmate. She ushered me — and with a genial smile on learning my name and errand— across a small square lobby into a room lighted by one window. I see the apartment now, vividly and in detail "in my mind's eye," and some remarks to follow will sufficiently explain why I enter into details. On the left side of the room and facing the window was a small chiffonnier, an article of furniture which for many years—and indeed still—in dwellings of modest pretensions filled the place and uses now accorded to a sideboard. On its slab-top were a few books.

Opposite the entering door was the fire-place, the mantel-shelf of which was decked with several figures or ornaments of common pottery-ware, flanked by two large sea-shells of gorgeous hues and dazzling lustre. At the side of the fire-place, between it and the window, was a stiff, old-fashioned, haircloth arm-chair — often misnamed an "easy" chair. Several chairs were ranged along the window side of the room, and in the window recess. Against the wall, facing the fire-place, was a sofa, I think haircloth. On one side of the sofa was the doorway entering from the little dark lobby. On the other side was a door-way giving admission to an inner room, of which I saw nothing. A small table with a pattern table-cover occupied the centre of the floor, which was carpeted. A few framed small engravings were hung on the walls. The whole betokened snug, cosy comfort; in short, what might be termed in Scottish vernacular a "snod" little room.

Causing me to be seated on the sofa, Mrs Lorimer said she expected my message, and " I'm ready for you." She then proceeded to draw me into conversation by questions as to my age, progress, and position at school, eliciting the fact,

en passant, that I was "dux" in my class, and had
recently gained a medal—"a *real silver* medal," as
I proudly emphasised, "with my name upon it, to
keep always to myself." "No, really!" said she,
pronouncing the word in a long drawn out "rālely"
—and now and again ejaculating, "Are you really?"
"Did you really?" in a kindly but half-bantering
tone, as I quickly perceived, together with the fact
that she was talking *down* to me as nurses talk
"baby talk" to their charges, so that each repetition of the hateful word "really" became more and
more painful, and I was growing shy, and decidedly
sulky. This she evidently saw, and suddenly
exclaiming, "But I'm forgetting, you've maybe no
had your dinner yet, and it's ill speaking between a
fou man and a fasting, ye ken;" and she abruptly
left for the inner room, from whence I heard the
sounds of locks and keys, indicative of her quick
movements. She soon re-entered, carrying a "bap"
(*Scottice,* not a scone, which is different and coarser),
a cup with jelly, and a small packet tied with tape,
sealed, and addressed to my father. She cut up
the "bap," spreading its two halves with a liberal
supply of jelly, which she assured me, *en parenthesis,*
was "real good." This word "real" and "really"

seemed to be continually in her mouth—"real
glad" and "really surprising" are among the
expressions on which she rung the changes, so that
gradually the objectionable bantering manner
seemed to fade away, and her speech, at the same
time, became more English or refined, and with
little tincture of common colloquialisms. She
urged me to eat, saying, "Dinna be blate, laddie,
dinna be blate, your teeth are longer than your
beard" — that being the last of the Scottish
vernacular I can recollect her using—"You'll soon
be a big man, you'll see," etc., etc. And here I may
comment—in an aside—that her reference to my
beard would be very inapplicable to my present
patriarchal aspect and condition. She soon succeeded in "wyling" me out of my incipient,
resentful shyness, and at last decidedly "scored"
in her kindly effort, when, after alluding with
apprehensiveness to the possible chances of my
being despoiled or of having the packet injured by
some of the big laddies, I was betrayed into a
vindicative assertion of my prowess in a narrative
of a very recent encounter with one of my schoolmates, "far older and bigger than myself," I
assured her, but in which "I licked him." "Did

you really?" she said, and this time in such a tone
of sympathetic admiration, patting me on the
shoulder, that, fairly won over by her blandish-
ments *and* by the "jeely piece," I got quite
loquacious and highly appreciative of the "bap,"
which, of course, I entirely finished.   She, however,
pointed out that there were other dangers against
which I should provide, such as the stone " bickers,"
or battles (*in memoriam*, I still carry a scar on my
head), which, in a normal condition of feud, were
so frequent in the Edinburgh of my boyhood
between the " puppies " and the " blackguards," as
the classes of male juveniles were distinctively
designated—the better class as prompt to resent
the name of " puppies " as the others cheerfully
accepted that of "blackguards."   They were, in
short, the Guelphs and the Ghibellines of the
juvenile male population of Edinburgh.   She
further slily hinted at dangers which might befall
me on some dark night from the "dumbie doctors "
—a sect of the healing art to whom, in the minds
of the rising generation, was attributed the practice
of lurking in common stairs, " closes," and "entries,"
shrouded in large, dark cloaks, and provided with
pitch plaisters, which they suddenly clapped over

the mouth and nose of an unwary, night-straggling urchin, stifling outcry and breath at the same moment, while the "dumbie doctor" enveloped his prey in the fearful black mantle, and swiftly hurried it off to the ever-yawning doors of "the dissecting-room." For this was within a few months of the time when the atrocities of Burke and Hare had been brought to the public knowledge, and were the theme of every tongue, and some of the victims, viz., "Daft Jamie" and "Bobby Aul," had been familiar objects to me. True, Burke had been hanged and Hare had disappeared from the city, but the great *Origo Mali* "Doctor Knox" was still looming largely to popular observation in his progress daily through the streets, and his physiognomy once seen was a never-to-be-forgotten one.

Here is a specimen of the street lyrics in which the "Burking affair" and the "Dumbie Doctors" were kept ever alive in the juvenile imagination :

> " William Burke and William Hare
> They cam' trotting doun the stair
> Wi' a Body in a Box
> For to sell to Doctor Knox ;
> Burke's the Butcher, Hare's the Thief,
> Knox the man that buys the beef."

C

I, of course, participated in the beliefs of "the horrible and awfu'" so prevalent among my congeners, with no forecasting that a time would come when in my close association with Dr Knox as his demonstrator, and from my familiarity with the actual arrangements of "the Practical Rooms," I would resent the possibility of his being in any way liable to the horrible odium under which he so suffered, or that I would aid my friend Dr Lonsdale with so much matter for his *Life of Knox, the Anatomist*, which illustrates the real disposition and character of the man. But Knox, while he lived, never got over the cloud thus cast upon him, although he was completely cleared in the eyes of the better informed through a special commission which scrutinised to the depths the existing usages and economy of the dissecting-room.

But to return from this digression into which I have almost unconsciously wandered while living over again my reminiscence of "Chloris." Mrs Lorimer having exhausted all topics in which we had mutual interest—or rather in which she could draw me out—I somewhat loath began my departure. But she held my hand long in motherly fashion, still plying with questions of my mother, sisters, and brothers; and finally and with kindly earnestness said, "Now, dinna forget when you are a big man that you had the good wish of the Lassie wi' the Lint-white Locks," touching her temples meaningly as she spoke, adding, and with one of her arch, sunny smiles, "Your father will tell you what I mean." I never have forgot, but in backward glances have often recalled the incident as a pleasing memory, and often recounted it to my children. And even now

> " My heart is idly stirred,
> For the same voice is in mine ear
> As in those days it heard."

On reaching home and delivering the packet I did not fail to tell my father of what she said, and he asked if I had noticed the colour of her hair. I said, "Yes, a very pretty colour," for I was *now* ready to vouch her pretty all over. My father then explained that the colour was called "flaxen," because flax, from which linen was made, was derived from lint, a plant with a white flower—that Mrs Lorimer was at one time called "The Lassie wi' the Lint-white Locks," from the light colour of her "flaxen" hair, "which had, however, a touch of yellow in it"—that she was very proud of her hair, and was pleased when its colour was observed. He then opened the packet, which, as I saw, contained several letters or writings, written, he said, "by Burns, the Poet," a friend of Mrs Lorimer's. On a subsequent occasion he told me that these papers were given to him in grateful acknowledgment of his professional services, Mrs L. not being "very well off," and he having declined to make any charge. For long afterwards these writings, with several others obtained from another source to which I will allude, were very familiar to my sight and to my handling, and that of others—too familiar indeed—for of the entire number, there remains only one accessible to me, and now lying before me—*i.e.*, "The Song of Death," which formed one of the enclosures in the packet referred to. It was given to, and preserved by my elder brother, Dr A. M. Adams, sometime Provost of Lanark. The MS. is now the property of his son, my nephew, Dr A. M. Adams, of Lanark, who prizes it because of its derivation, and because of its being a favourite of his father and grandfather. To this special MS. I will again make reference, as it has the first line written on it of another poem by Burns, and the

words written furnish me a peg on which I purpose
to hang a few critical comments apropos of imperfect versions and erroneous records of the works
of Burns. (Appendix, Note B, p. 151.) The additional writings of Burns which came into my father's
possession, and subject to my handling, were given
him by another patient, bearing a name familiar
in all the biographies of Burns. She was a Mrs
Findlater, and was the widow of the son or
nephew—I forget which—of Mr Findlater of the
Excise, long a colleague of Burns, and his
immediate superior officer in the service. This
lady resided in Rankeillor Street, Newington, and
her son Duff was my playfellow and companion
for some time, especially on Saturday afternoons,
which I frequently passed in his mother's cosy
kitchen, there to partake among other joys of a
most delicious gingerbread of her own baking.
The recollections of that incomparable gingerbread are as enduring as that of Mrs Lorimer's
"bap" and "jeely."

Mrs Findlater had a large number of Burns's
writings in her possession or custody, and they
lay with little care in a large table desk of plain
fir — probably an old office desk — being freely

accessible to Duff and myself. Indeed, as the paper was stout and peculiarly suitable, we frequently used the unwritten sides of the sheets for our artistic aspirations in delineating houses, beasts, and boats. The peculiarities of the handwriting I have a much stronger recollection of than I have of the subjects of the poems; but both were as familiar to my observation as the pages of the *Shorter Catechism* or of *Lennie's Grammar*, and as little valued. But with the character of the handwriting I am so interpenetrated that I fancy I could, even now, enter the witness-box with Craibe Angus himself as an expert. Not only was the writing as characteristic and cognoscible as a man's features are, the paper itself was of distinctive qualities. Stiff and rough on surface, usually with one or more ragged edges, as if from a half-sheet being torn or cut across or as if dragged out of a book, which was indeed the case, as we were told they had been taken from old Excise ledgers. They were often ruled in peculiar fashion with perpendicular lines — no doubt to suit office forms—and the ruling was in faint red. Often the paper bore official stamps, and we frequently puzzled to make out the meaning of the water mark. From the little care given, Mrs Findlater did not seem to set much store on them; probably their plenty and familiarity had bred indifference. And even in the case of my father the truth of the proverb "Lightly come, lightly gone" was well exemplified in the winnowing process through which in time . his "routh" of Burns's poetic gear passed into the hands of more appreciative and longer-sighted borrowers and appropriators, is shown in the solitary sample now the property of my nephew. The course of a number of the missing MSS. was subsequently traced at a time when their priceless value was better understood. Thus, a lot were borrowed by a friend of my father, who did not carry out his *intention*—of which there is no doubt—to have them published in fac-simile, with others which had come into the gentleman's possession. But for some time before his death, which occurred between the "fifties" and the "sixties," he had got so weakened in mind as to need being led about by a caretaker; and, as was explained to me by his representative, it was not known, and could not be traced, what had become of them — only known that they were

not in the possession of his executors. Any
attempt at their recovery was therefore not
only a distasteful but clearly an impracticable
task. I could tell of one or two MSS. that
passed foolishly from my own hands, and regarding which "sorrow's memory is sorrow still."

About thirty years after this—to me memorable
incident of my interview with "Chloris"—there
occurred the centenary celebrations of 1859,
among the most important of which was the
great banquet in the City Hall, Glasgow, of
which I was a delighted participant. On the
day following I was in Edinburgh, and had
reunion with my father, with whom the evening
was passed in a delightful "twa-handed crack,"
the main burden of our discourse being Burnsiana.
We discussed the all-over-world events of the
preceding evening—the speeches at the Glasgow
banquet of Sir Archibald Alison, Glassford
Bell, Norman Macleod, Samuel Lover, Colonel
Burns, the son of the poet, etc., etc.; and we
naturally reverted to Mrs Lorimer. I rehearsed
my impressions and had confirmed my recollections of her as compared with his better
knowledge, but they were so confirmed and

identical with his that I could not now separate what I may have incorporated as my very own.

I will describe as well as I may her physical aspect as she was impressed on the plastic basis, but enduringly solidified mould, of my boyish memory. The words of Burns, "Bonie, blooming, straight, and tall," will seem incongruous to the reader, as she was no longer young as when Burns so described her; but discounting the two first words, and substituting "fresh and comely," they would still be appropriate to my conception as it now exists. Her countenance has been in frequent varied phraseology described as bewitchingly lovely. To me it was only very pleasing. Her hair, abundant, was of what I should at the present time indicate as of a pale straw, yellowish lemon colour of glossy sheen, parted in the centre, and disposed on each side in spiral rolls or coils— not, I think, naturally curly, nor were they corkscrew curls, the product of iron tongs, but such as may be formed by twirling the hair round the fingers and fixing with paper or hairpins. There were, I think, two coils falling on each side of the face. Her head was enclosed—not merely topped—in greater part by "a mutch" (*Scottice*),

D

the border "goffered," not crimped or plaited, and
with tie ribbons pendant, not fastened under the
chin, but fluttering loosely with the curls. This
"mutch" was a something "wide as the poles
asunder" from the dainty little article of ivy leaf
dimensions seen nowadays perched on the crown of
the heads of natty hospital nurses, probationers, or
house and table maids. The contour of the frilled
border I have been reminded of by some portraits
of Mary Queen of Scots. Her features I will not
attempt to describe further than to say that her
eyes were full, the eyebrows of a decidedly darker
colour than the hair and what I may call "bushy,"
and the expression of the eyes was arch and lively.
But my entire impression of her face is that of
an effect, not referable to eyes, nose, or mouth—

> 'Tis not an eye, or lip, we beauty call,
> But the joint force and full result of all ;

an effect, indeed, far better conceived from Burns's
description—

> " Sae flaxen were her ringlets,
>   Her eyebrows of a darker hue,
> Bewitchingly o'er-arching
>   Twa laughing een o' lovely blue :
> Her smiling, sae wyling,
>   Wad make a wretch forget his woe ;
> What pleasure, what treasure,
>   Unto these rosy lips to grow ! "

an effect exemplified in the charming wiling manner in which she wiled a shy boy from his sulky mood into that of happy *abandon* and boyish confidence. Her voice was pleasing, "soft, and low," while her speech was of the Scottish vernacular, then so universal in Edinburgh, but her accent and pronunciation were different, very different, from that familiar to me in the speech of my schoolmates, of servant maids, or of such society of grown-up persons as I had access to. of any of my readers have had opportunities of conversing with an Inverness or a Dublin lady speaking pure English, and can contrast their impressions with those they have experienced when conversing with a Cockney London lady, they will understand what I wish to convey of difference in her dialect from that of the Edinburgh ordinary vernacular. As a boy, while still in sharp mind regarding some details, I can only recall general impressions. What she must have been in her youth I have ofttimes tried to imagine.

I saw her when she was old, although with little sign of age to my eyes, but still above fifty—say fifty-four years. She was, and had been ailing,

although not in any way observable by me. On the
contrary, she seemed fresh and well preserved—
neither stout nor thin, but "tall and straight" and
even "blooming," and to my boyish apprehension
she realised one impression that Burns's description
has burnt in upon me. "Like harmony her
motion," are his words, and that I realised as
"smooth gliding without step" she passed to and
from the apartment. As to her height, I am aided
in conjecture by an external stimulus to memory.
Most people must be conscious that a chance word,
odour, or object will at times open the caverns
of memory, and forms and incidents are evoked
that had long slumbered in total oblivion. There
is of my acquaintance a lady whom I see occasionally, and I am sometimes startled at the
manner in which she reminds me of Chloris.
If I might parody a passage from the Bard of
Memory, I would say—

> " As kindred objects kindred thoughts inspire,
>   As summer clouds shoot forth electric fire,
>   So does one form recall a form I knew,
>   Warm as with life, and, like the mirror, true."

On a late occasion I was tempted to ask this
lady her height; she replied—"Five feet seven

inches," and that is my estimate of the height of Jean Lorimer.

"But how was she dressed?" asks some lady. That involves an answer for which I am dubious. I noted her "mutch," because it seemed a part of her face, on which my gaze was mainly fixed. I am certain, however, that her gown was of a bright colour, short in the waist, and high up on the neck, but of what stuff or of what pattern, or of any pattern, or how "cut" I still cannot say. Neither can I tell if her sleeves were *bishop, gigot,* or *coat,* but regarding the skirt I can make affidavit that she did not wear crinoline. Like Troy's proud dames, her garments "swept the ground." That she was shod I infer, but whether in boots, shoes, or slippers, high heels or low heels, I did not see or look.

For some time prior to the date of this conversation with my father, I had been incited, by the approaching centenary celebrations, to a diligent reading of the life and works of Burns, more specially as presented in the library edition of Robert Chambers (1857), in four volumes, and I had been greatly interested and troubled with a passage in his record of Jean Lorimer, whom he

.usually calls Mrs Whelpdale, although she entirely
gave up her married name after being deserted by
her husband.   Chambers deals with her history
in a truthful, generous, and kindly sympathetic
spirit, and only to one passage in her pitiful story
can I make exception to his references to this
lady—for she was a lady in her manner and in
her early position in life.   "It is understood," he
says, "that this poor, unprotected woman at length
was led into an error which lost her the respect
of society.   She spent some time in a kind of
vagrant life, verging on mendicancy. . . . She
never ceased to be elegant in her form and comely
of. face, nor did she ever cease to remember that
she had been the subject of some dozen compositions by one of the greatest modern masters of
the lyre," etc.   This passage troubled me, and I
questioned my father as likely to know the truth
regarding the alleged vagrant life, the mendicancy
and abject poverty conveyed in these references,
and especially the "error" which "at length"
had lost her the respect of society.   My father
answered quickly and almost with angry earnestness—"Not at all ; nothing of the kind ; these are
ungenerous aspersions on the good name of an

unhappy and much misunderstood lady, originat-
ing no doubt in entire ignorance. Contradict
them wherever you hear them." He then went
into much detail of the early and later life of
Miss Lorimer so far as known to and gathered
by him, and he felt assured he had little to learn.
The main facts were as given by Chambers, and
since confirmed or in entire accordance with the
latest, and out of all question the foremost,
authority on all that concerns Burns—viz., Mr
Scott Douglas. He explained that Miss Lorimer's
father was a substantial farmer and also a somewhat extensive merchant, who, unfortunate in
business, lost all, and became a broken man while
his daughter was little beyond her twenty-first year.
She had been inveigled into a foolish love marriage
(March 1793) while under eighteen years, and was
abandoned after a few weeks by her contemptible
scamp of a husband, a spendthrift young farmer,*
whom she never again saw for a period of twenty-
three years, and then only by chance, when she

---

* Allan Cunningham, with characteristic inaccuracy, *or unveracity*,
for both were his characteristics, says that Chloris's husband, a
"southron, name of Whelpdale," was "an officer of the army."
He was no more an officer of the army than was Burns, or
Cunningham himself. (Appendix, Note C, p. 164.)

heard of him as a prisoner in Carlisle, eking out
his ne'er-do-weel existence to its unprofitable end.
After her father's failure Miss Lorimer had no
shelter, and was without means. She was unfit for
menial country labour, and had to betake herself
to plain governessing, needlework, or such shifty,
precarious occupations as were then open to
women's employment. Necessarily in this strag-
gling, cheerless course of struggle she had to
change her residence, and only because of such a
struggle for bare subsistence could she be made
liable to the improper phrasing of vagrancy or
mendicancy. When at length, in 1822, she sought
an abiding place in Edinburgh, her history was
communicated to the public through the papers
of the day, and among the various notices elicited
there were none that in the slightest affected her
moral character. On the contrary, there was
evoked a disposition to aid, and friends gathered,
touched by what was always so obvious of her
gentle, amiable disposition and her evil fortunes.
Much of the interest elicited was no doubt due to
what was known of the high respect in which she
had ever been held and spoken of by Burns,
who had carefully discriminated between her and

many others of his female friends, the objects of his poetical inspirations. She ultimately became housekeeper to a highly-respected gentleman whom my father knew, a resident in Newington, who continued her friend while she lived. His house, as my father reminded me, he had pointed out in the course of an evening walk while traversing one of the wooded avenues which connect the east side of Newington with the Castle o' Clouts, or Powburn Road, leading to Echo Bank Cemetery. Blacket Place, I think, the avenue was called. Mrs Lorimer's health latterly gave way, and she became unfit for housekeeping duties, and she was settled by her kind employer in the little house where I saw her, and where she lived till the end in decent comfort, able "to do her own turns" till near the last. Her wants and comforts were eked out by a number of well-dispositioned persons, chiefly ladies, who commiserated her lonely lot. My father had never known her spoken of in disparaging terms, and there had never been communicated to him by any Mrs Grundy whisperings past or present as existing among her neighbours, of whom he knew many of a kind who would not be slow to communicate.

I need scarcely say how much gratification this testimony of my father's gave me at the time, and has since remained with me, by dispelling utterly the uncomfortable impressions conveyed in Chambers's ill-considered utterance—one of what Scott Douglas terms his "thoughtless" statements, for which then, nor since, has any real cause been shown. Indeed, from the entire context of Chambers's story, and the absolute nullity of any hint as to the error so vaguely indicated, I am well satisfied that the only error of which he was cognisant, and which was in his mind when he penned the words "at length" instead of "at first," was the early, the beginning step of her hasty, foolish marriage, which led her otherwise happy course of life astray. As regards her relations with Burns he speaks most generously, therein in unison with Scott Douglas's investigations, and in repudiation of Allan Cunningham's rank, weedy imaginations, upholds Chloris's walk and conversation as blameless from "the time she came more specially under the notice of Burns, in the full blaze of her uncommon beauty," and says that with the feelings of "the poetical admirer there appears to have been mingled the compassionate tenderness due to the hapless fate of his young heroine." Her father, says Chambers, had realised some wealth, and, in addition to farming, carried on extensive mercantile transactions in Dumfries and at his residence at Kemmis Hall.

"It was in consequence of his dealing in teas and spirits that he fell under the attention of the poet, who then protected the Revenue interests in ten parishes. Burns became intimate with the Lorimers. They scarcely ever had company at their house without inviting him ; they often sent him delicacies from their farm, and whenever he passed their way on his professional tours Mrs Lorimer was delighted to minister to his comforts with a basin of tea or whatever else he might please to have. A daughter of the family recollects seeing many letters of his addressed to her father ; one contained only the words, ' Coming, sir,' a quaint answer to some friendly note of invitation," etc.

Chambers continues the history of Jean Lorimer till the period when her husband

"was obliged by his debts to remove hastily from Barnhill, leaving his young wife no resource but that of returning to her parents at Kemmis Hall. She saw her husband no more for twenty-three years."

Burns's "intimacy with the 'Kemmis Hall' family was kept up—and, let it be remarked, he was not intimate with them merely as an individual, but as the head of a family, for his wife was as much the

friend and associate of the Lorimers as himself,
though perhaps less frequently at their house."

I beg my readers to bear with me a little longer
while placing the nature of Chloris's relations with
the poet in their true aspect, because an endeavour
was made in Allan Cunningham's edition to obscure
those relations by stating that Chloris was a person
who as a beauty thought "that love should be
under no demure restraint," and " rewarded Burns
by giving him many opportunities of catching
inspiration from her presence," etc., etc., *ad nauseam*.
But Scott Douglas, referring to the insinuation, says
—" We do not know what was Allan Cunningham's
authority for this passage regarding poor Chloris,"
and in his full note epitomising the history of
Chloris, he gives 3rd August 1795—about a year
before Burns's death—as that on which the poet

"sent to Thomson two of his very finest songs, of which
'Chloris' is the theme, and up to this time she continued to
be the mistress of his musings, if not of his heart. . . .
Within a day or two after these songs were posted to
Thomson, an Edinburgh gentleman for whom Burns had a
high respect, and who was a great enthusiast in Scottish
minstrelsy, Mr Robert Cleghorn, paid him a visit at
Dumfries, accompanied by two friends, Mr Wight and Mr
Allan, one or both of whom were also farmers. Our poet
resolved to give them an entertainment in his own house,
and Jean Lorimer and her father were invited to meet them

there. It is thus very satisfactory to know that his inter-
course with Chloris was of no clandestine character. At
that meeting Mrs Burns could not fail to delight the
company with her 'wood notes wild,' giving effect to some
of the very songs which 'Chloris' had inspired. It appears
certain that she did *sing one of these* ['O, that's the lassie
o' my heart'], a fresh effusion to the beautiful tune 'Morag,'
which so delighted Cleghorn that on his return to Edinburgh
he wrote for a copy of it."

Mr Douglas gives the letter of invitation, for the
first time published, and interesting as illustrating the
terms of intimacy existing between Jean Lorimer's
family and that of Burns. The letter is addressed
"To Mr Wm. Lorimer, Senior, Farmer," and begins:

" My dear Sir,—I called for you yesternight both at your
own house and at your favourite lady's—Mrs Hyslop of the
Globe—but could not find you. I want you to dine with me
to-day. I have two honest Mid-Lothian farmers with me,
who have travelled threescore miles to renew old friendship
with the poet; and I promise you a pleasant party, a plateful
of hotch-potch, and a bottle of good sound port. Mrs Burns
desired me yesternight to beg the favour of Jeanie to come
and partake, and she was so obliging as to promise that she
would. Jeanie and you [Mr Syme, Dr Maxwell, and Dr
Mundell] are all the people besides my Edinburgh friends
whom I wish to see, and if you can come I shall take it very
kind.—Yours,   "ROBT. BURNS.
" (Dinner at three.)"

"The above," continues Mr Douglas, "proves
the intimacy that existed between the poet's

family and that of the Lorimers, and indicates, moreover, that the tenderness evinced by Burns for Chloris was *of no clandestine kind.*"

So much for the relations existing between Burns and Chloris. On 3rd August 1795, Burns presented to her a book on which he wrote the last poem he dedicated to her, and headed it with the following :—" Inscription, written on the blank leaf of a copy of the last edition of my poems, presented to the lady whom, in so many fictitious reveries of passion, but with the most ardent sentiments of real friendship, I have so often sung under the name of 'Chloris.'" Then follows the poem commencing—

"'Tis friendship's pledge, my young fair friend."

"Poor 'Chloris' henceforth disappears from the scene. Within twelve short months after this period," writes Scott Douglas, "the heart of her minstrel ceased to beat, and his lyre was for ever unstrung. Her father sank into poverty, and she became a cheerless wanderer. The last seven years of her life were passed in Edinburgh. A few friends turned up for her in that city, and there still exists an affecting note in her handwriting, return-ing thanks for some little kindnesses bestowed. The words are these :—' Burns's Chloris is infinitely obliged to Mrs —— for her kind attention in sending the newspapers, and feels pleased and flattered by having so much said and done on her behalf. Ruth was kindly and generously treated by Boaz ; perhaps Burns's Chloris may enjoy a similar fate in the fields of men of talent and worth.— March 2, 1825.'"

Referring to this note, in which Chambers says :

"'We cannot help thinking there is something not unworthy of a poetical heroine. . . . The lady here addressed saw Mrs Whelpdale [Chloris] several times, and was pleased with her conversation, which showed considerable native acuteness of understanding, and a play of wit such as might have been supposed to charm a high intellect in one of the opposite sex.' . . . Poor Chloris is a sad memento of the evils which, under the existing usages of society, spring to woman *from one rash step* in what is for that sex the most important movement in life. Life was to her *clouded in its morn*. Every grace that heaven gives to make woman a charm and a solace to man was possessed in vain ; all through this false step, taken though it was at a time when she could scarcely be considered as responsible for her own actions."

Actum ne agas seems whispering in my ear while I write, yet although I fear I *am* overdoing it, I cannot refrain, in closing my present reference to Chloris's character and relations to Burns and to her contemptible husband of a few weeks, by reminding my readers that Ruth was treated kindly and generously because, in the words recorded in Scripture, she "was a virtuous woman," and because, as there shown, she was

a pattern of fidelity to the highest duties. There
can surely be none who think it possible that
while inquiries and representations were being
publicly made in Edinburgh, an intelligent woman
like Jean Lorimer would pose herself before a
lady of her own sex, and before "men of talent
and genius," such as abounded in the Metropolis,
and invite a contrast between herself and Ruth,
heedless of the result.

She suffered much from severe "winter cough"
(chronic bronchitis), and died September 1831—
aged fifty-six years. She was interred in Newington Burying Ground. She was born in 1775
at Craigieburn House, near Moffat.

Before drawing attention to a list of Burns's
poems which are associated with the name of
Chloris, I note emphatically that there exist in
her case no trace of such writings, whether in prose
or in verse, as characterise the Clarinda correspondence. None whatever. Nevertheless Allan
Cunningham has written of her thus:

"The beauty of Chloris has added many charms to
Scottish song. But that which increased the reputation of
the poet has lessened that of the man. Chloris was one of
those who believe in the dispensing power of beauty, and
thought that love should be under no demure restraint.

Burns sometimes thought in the same way himself; and it is not wonderful, therefore, that the poet should celebrate the charms of a liberal beauty who was willing to reward his strains, and who gave him many opportunities of catching inspiration from her presence. The poet gave many a glowing picture of her youth, health, and voluptuous beauty, but let no lady envy the poetical elevation of poor Chloris; her situation in poetry is splendid; her situation in life merits our pity—perhaps our charity."

The situation of poor Chloris when this man penned this slander was that of rest in her grave. She died about two years previous, and she left no male relative to give the libeller the thrashing he so richly merited. This is the passage in justification for which Scott Douglas records that he could find "*no authority*," and that neither Cunningham nor any other has given the smallest item of warranty for. I never see the passage without being reminded of Byron's " sketch " of one who was

> " Skilled with a touch to deepen scandal's tint
> With all the deep mendacity of hint ;
> And mingling truth with falsehood, sneers with smiles,
> A thread of candour with a web of wiles."

But here there *was no scandal* other than in the man's *mendacious hint—" the effort of his own imagination."* He was a versatile writer, but in some of his writings he reminds one of the octopus, which emits an inky fluid that makes

F

the waters turbid, and enables the creature to
hide itself in the mud. He wielded a facile
pen, but notoriously drew on his imagination for
his facts—*a fact* for which he has been pilloried by
his contemporaries.   (Appendix, Note B, p. 151,
and Note C, p. 164.) Hogg, the Ettrick Shepherd,
who was his very intimate friend and admirer, says :

" I was astonished at the luxuriousness of his fancy. *It
was boundless*, but it was the luxury of a rich garden
overrun with rampant weeds. . . . When once he
began, it was impossible to calculate where or when he was
going to end."

Scott Douglas, who was by no means "mealy-
mouthed" in his references to men or women
associated with the life and works of Burns, but
who " nothing extenuates, nor aught sets down in
malice," says, after recording Cunningham's chart
of the qualifications he boasted himself possessed
of, as " amusing," adds that Allan Cunningham's
labours on Burns's Life and Works " are now
regarded as practically worthless by readers *who
prefer honest fact to fiction;*" and further on,
referring to a picturesque description given by
Cunningham of certain incidents as occurring
under his personal observation, says it was only a
" lively effort of fancy," and that it might well be

doubted, if he had lived in the locality referred to. Chambers, who made special investigations into certain incidents narrated in detail by Cunningham, thinking no doubt that the proper place for finding out the truth of a rumour was in the place where the rumour was said to have occurred, says that he, Cunningham, had made "extraordinary porridge" of these incidents of the poet's life, and that indeed he believed Cunningham had "never set a foot in Ayrshire."

Cunningham, it must be admitted, was a charming writer, but therein the more dangerous. For, like Joseph Surface, he was—as may be noted in the passage on which I am commenting—given to utter "noble sentiments," for does he not emit the sentiment that Chloris, because of her "situation in life," merits our pity—perhaps our charity! and states that one of the most creditable, most honourable, utterly blameless episodes in the life of Burns, had, while increasing the reputation of the poet, "lessened that of the man." . With Sir Peter Teazle, I say "damn his sentiments!"

It should be clearly evident that Cunningham, with his foul, weedy imagination, was little capable of discriminating the imaginings of others, whether

men or women, and quite unfit to recognise the
"white flower love" which Gilbert Burns says did
truly characterise the love his brother had for
many of his divinities of song — such love as
Burns himself describes as purely "fictitious," the
idealised incarnation of a poet's imaginings — a
love *ex gratia* such as inspired the charming poem
of the "Lass o' Ballochmyle" (Miss Alexander).
This lady, with whom the poet never in his life
exchanged one word, and whom he by mere
chance encountered in his evening walk—looked
at earnestly—as she passed on "in maiden meditation fancy free," and thereupon wrote and sent her
his delightful song, accompanied with a corresponding complimentary letter. In that song he
depicts himself as one who would—

> "With rapture toil,
> And nightly to my bosom strain
> The bonie lass o' Ballochmyle."

This compliment the "lass" did not deign to
even acknowledge. Possibly she may have had a
taint of that gross literality of conception which
pervaded Cunningham's rankly luxuriant and
weedy imagination. But in failing to recognise
the genius of the "fool she met i' the forest," and

who was ignorant or unmindful of the *convenances* due to her *superior* " situation in life," she had no conception in her scornful pride that save for this poem the world would never have known that she had ever existed. But the time did come when she was proud to exhibit both letter and poem, carefully preserved in a. glass case, and with no apprehensiveness of incurring from some Mrs Grundy or a Cunningham their " pity—perhaps charity."

PART II.

IT may now fairly be asked what are the compositions of Burns that evoke an interest in the personality of Chloris, that are associated with, and in which he gave evidence of the sentiments inspired by his poetic model? Robert Chambers, in his Library (4 vols., 1857) Edition, which is by far the best up to the date, speaks of "*eleven* songs," which he, however, does not altogether clearly indicate, and some of those he gives are imperfect through negligent omissions. Other editions give a few in a haphazard fashion, but Scott Douglas's edition (6 vols., 1891) is beyond challenge the most comprehensive, the fullest in detail, the most complete and accurate in giving the latest versions approved by Burns, together with earlier versions and emendations, and also the most authoritative in its thorough verification of dates, alleged incidents, etc. From Scott Douglas's work I have no difficulty in drawing out a list of thirty poems attributable to Chloris, to which *doubtfully* an additional one may be added. And as this magnificent edition can only be accessible to some of my readers, I think it will be a gratification to many to have a record list—an index as it were, and an opportunity of comparing that list with such copy of Burns as may be at their command, thus ascertaining the fulness or shortcomings of their own book of reference. In this list I will give the titles *as given by Burns*, which often differ from those employed by his editors. These titles, with the verses, will facilitate reference and identification.

I. CRAIGIEBURN WOOD.

"This song," says Burns, "was composed on a passion which a Mr Gillespie, a particular friend of mine, had for a Miss Lorimer, afterwards Mrs Whelpdale. The young lady was born at Craigieburn Wood. The chorus is part of an old, foolish ballad." In a letter to Thomson he says he got it —that is, the old foolish song and air—taken down from a country girl's singing. It is called "Craigieburn Wood," and, in the opinion of Mr Clarke, is one of our sweetest "Scots songs." Mr Thomson objected strongly to the chorus, as rendering the song quite inadmissible where ladies were present, and Mr Stephen Clarke wrote:

"There is no need to mention the chorus. The man who would attempt to sing a chorus to this beautiful air should have his throat cut to prevent him from doing it again."

Burns, in reply to Thomson's criticism, writes:

"In fact the chorus *was* not my work, but part of some old verses to the air. If I can catch myself in a more than ordinary propitious moment I shall write a new 'Craigieburn' altogether. My heart is much in the theme."

The song (*wanting the chorus*) follows :—

Sweet closes the ev'ning on Craigieburn Wood,
    And blythely awakens the morrow;
But the pride o' the spring on the Craigieburn Wood
    Can yield me nought but sorrow.

I see the spreading leaves and flowers,
    I hear the wild birds singing;
But pleasure they hae nane for me,
    While care my heart is wringing.

I canna tell, I maunna tell,
    I daurna for your anger;
But secret love will break my heart,
    If I conceal it langer:

I see thee gracefu', straight, and tall,
    I see thee sweet and bonie;
But oh, what will my torment be
    If thou refuse thy Johnie!

To see thee in another's arms,
  In love to lie and languish,
'Twad be my dead, that will be seen,
  My heart wad burst wi' anguish.

But Jeanie, say thou wilt be mine,
  Say thou lo'es nane before me ;
And a' my days o' life to come,
  I'll gratefully adore thee.

When I come to speak of the second and finally approved version of "Craigieburn" which Burns did carry into effect, his heart being in the theme, I may be tempted to tell a story of a piece of vicarious wooing which I all unintentionally, but with better success than Burns, effected in the case of a young couple.

2. O POORTITH CAULD AND RESTLESS LOVE.

TUNE—"*Cauld Kail in Aberdeen.*"

This song was composed in 1793, two or three months before the marriage of Miss Lorimer, and one of the verses, and indeed the whole song, was, as Mr Douglas suggests, like the preceding, a piece of vicarious wooing in aid of his friend Gillespie, a fellow-officer in the Excise :

G

O POORTITH cauld, and restless love,
    Ye wrack my peace between ye;
Yet poortith a' I could forgive
    An 'twerna for my Jeanie.

Chorus—O why should Fate such pleasure have
      Life's dearest bands untwining?
    Or why sae sweet a flower as love
      Depend on fortune's shining?*

The warld's wealth, when I think on,
    Its pride, and a' the lave o't;
O fie a silly coward man,
    That he should be the slave o't!

Her e'en, sae bonie blue betray
    How she repays my passion;
But prudence is her o'er word ay,
    She talks o' rank and fashion.

O wha can prudence think upon,
    And sic a lassie by him?
O wha can prudence think upon
    And sae in love as I am?

The verse suggested by Mr Douglas is—

    "Her e'en, sae bonie blue betray
      How she repays my passion;
    But prudence is her o'er word ay,
      She talks o' rank and fashion."

* Our poet subsequently cancelled the repetition of the second stanza *as a chorus*, and preferred that it should remain as a verse of the song.

Poor girl, she had hopes of "rank and fashion" through her dandy scamp of a husband.

Burns was not satisfied with this fine song, and vowed to make a better to the same tune and on the same lady he had attempted to celebrate in the words of "Poortith Cauld." This he did a few months after by producing the following :—

3. COME, LET ME TAKE THEE TO MY BREAST.

TUNE—"*Cauld Kail.*"

COME, let me take thee to my breast,
　　And pledge we ne'er shall sunder;
And I shall spurn as vilest dust
　　The world's wealth and grandeur :
And do I hear my Jeanie own
　　That equal transports move her ?
I ask, for dearest life alone,
　　That I may live to love her.

Thus in my arms, wi' a' her charms,
　　I clasp my countless treasure;
I'll seek nae mair o' Heav'n to share
　　Than sic a moment's pleasure :
And by thy e'en, sae bonie blue,
　　I swear I'm thine for ever;
And on thy lips I seal my vow,
　　And break it shall I never !

Thomson would not gratify the poet by setting
the preceding song, "Poortith Cauld," which Burns
had penned in celebration of Jean Lorimer; and
again he thwarted the bard by setting this song to
the far inferior Irish air, "Alley Croker" (although
Burns did not live to become aware of his correspondent's perversity), despite of Burns telling
him—"For private reasons I wish to see this
song in print. If it suits you to insert it I
shall be pleased, as the heroine is a favourite
of mine."

Some of my readers may think it probable that
Jean Armour was the "Jeanie" of this song of
"Poortith Cauld," but Jean Armour's eyes were
"jet, jet black an' like a Hawk," while Jean
Lorimer's were, as he so frequently reminds us,
"bonie blue."

4. WHISTLE AND I'LL COME TO YE, MY LAD.

This unique song was inspired by the charms
of Jean Lorimer (late Mrs Whelpdale). Burns
instructed Thomson to alter the closing line of
the chorus to "Thy Jeanie will venture wi' ye,
my jo"; and he added—"In fact, a fair dame,

whom the Graces have attired in witchcraft, and whom the Loves have armed with lightning—a fair one, *herself the heroine of the song*, insists on the amendment, and dispute her commands if you dare." This order was issued on 5th August 1795, two years after the song was composed, but recalled in February 1796. The song goes thus:

Chorus—O WHISTLE an' I'll come to ye, my lad,
　　　　　　O whistle an' I'll come to ye, my lad;
　　　　　　Tho' father and mother an' a' should gae mad,
　　　　　　O whistle an' I'll come to ye, my lad.

But warily tent when ye come to court me,
And come nae unless the back-yett be a-jee;
Syne up the back-style, and let naebody see,
And come as ye werena comin to me,
And come as ye werena comin to me.

At kirk, or at market, whene'er ye meet me,
Gang by me as tho' that ye car'd na' a flie;
But steal me a blink o' your bonie black ee,
Yet look as ye werena lookin' to me,
Yet look as ye werena lookin' to me.

　　　　　O whistle and I'll come, etc.

In a footnote, Dr Currie says he has "heard the heroine of the song sing it herself, in the very

spirit of arch simplicity which it requires."
Cunningham and Motherwell held that Mrs *Maria*
Riddell laid claim to be the heroine, "rather an
odd confession to proceed from a married lady."
Burns refused Thomson's insistent petition that
"the charming Jeanie" would let the line remain
unaltered (that is, would exclude "Thy Jeanie
will venture wi' ye, my jo"), and insisted that
the heroine herself wished the name as given,
"and dispute her commands if you dare." As
Scott Douglas says in summing up the con-.
troversy, "the author of the song ought to have
known that matter best," and "that this song
was inspired by the charms of Jean Lorimer
(late Mrs Whelpdale) cannot admit of a doubt."
The only variation attempted was in the chorus,
regarding which Thomson wrote in vain urging
Burns to "petition the charming Jeanie to
let the chorus of *Whistle and I'll come to ye,
my lad*, remain unaltered," instead of Jeanie's
version, viz. :

> "O whistle and I'll come to ye, my jo,
>   O whistle and I'll come to ye, my jo ;
>   Tho' father and mother an' a' should say no,
>   Thy Jeanie will venture wi' ye, my jo."

5. SHE SAYS SHE LO'ES ME BEST OF A'.

TUNE—"*Oonagh's Waterfall.*"

Of this song, commencing "Sae flaxen were her ringlets," I have already given the first eight lines when describing Mrs Lorimer's personal appearance.

SAE flaxen were her ringlets,
　　Her eyebrows of a darker hue,
Bewitchingly o'er-arching
　　Twa laughing een o' lovely blue :
Her smiling, sae wyling,
　　Wad make a wretch forget his woe ;
What pleasure, what treasure,
　　Unto these rosy lips to grow !
Such was my Chloris' bonie face,
　　When first that bonie face I saw ;
And ay my Chloris' dearest charm—
　　She says she lo'es me best of a'.

Like harmony her motion,
　　Her pretty ankle is a spy,
Betraying fair proportion,
　　Wad make a saint forget the sky :
Sae warming, sae charming,
　　Her fautless form and gracefu' air ;
Ilk feature—auld Nature
　　Declar'd that she could do nae mair ;
Her's are the willing chains o' Love,
　　By conquering Beauty's sovereign law ;

And still my Chloris' dearest charm—
    She says, she lo'es me best of a'.

Let others love the City,
    And gaudy show, at sunny noon ;
Gie me the lonely valley,
    The dewy eve and rising moon ;
Fair beaming, and streaming,
    Her silver light the boughs amang ;
While falling, recalling,
    The amorous thrush concludes his sang ;
There, dearest Chloris, wilt thou rove
    By wimpling burn and leafy shaw,
And hear my vows o' truth and love,
    And say, thou lo'es me best of a'?

Thomson, in acknowledging receipt of the song, says "It is one of the pleasantest table songs I have seen, and henceforth shall be mine when the song is going round."

Above fifty years back, in my singing days, and when the song was going round, it was also mine, not alone because of the delightful melody, and characteristic sample of Burns pre-eminence as a national song-writer, as because it opened the eyelids of memory, and renewed a "blink" of the well-remembered heroine who flitted in the sunshine of the past. (Appendix, Note D, p. 167.)

6. ON CHLORIS REQUESTING ME TO GIVE HER
A SPRIG OF BLOSSOMED THORN.

FROM the white-blossomed sloe my dear Chloris
    requested
  A sprig, her fair breast to adorn :
No, by Heavens! I exclaim'd, let me perish, if ever
  I plant in that bosom a thorn !

This poetic gem, termed by Burns a "clench,"
and struck, as it were, by one stroke of the
hammer from out the mine of a poet's inspiration, has a somewhat curious history. My
readers will look in vain for it in any edition
of Burns save that of Scott Douglas, where, for
the first time, it is included in its true position.
It seems that it was one of seventeen short
poems forwarded by Burns to Creech, bookseller, in 1795 to be included in the early
volume of his works, then being printed in
Edinburgh. Creech did not include it, but
kept it by him. But copies had got into cir-
culation, and one reaching the hands of Shield,
a performer in the orchestra of a London
theatre, and also a music composer, he set the

H

lines to an air of his own and had it issued
in sheet-music form with another verse linked
to give the song reasonable length.   It is
alleged that the added lines are by Dibdin ;
but, however this may be, the song got into
vogue and was sung by Incledon, Braham, and
others, and has since found a place in a
thousand song books and music books under
the name of " The Thorn," being ascribed to
the authorship variously of W. Shield (who
composed the music), of Incledon, Braham, and
others (who sang it), of O'Keefe (who had
nothing good, bad, or indifferent to do with
it), but never ascribed to Burns.   But this I
must correct, for only a few days back I saw
in a quarto song book, with music, termed *110
National Songs*—publisher, Cameron, Glasgow—
the song, to which is attached a footnote to
the effect that it has been supposed by some
to have been written by Burns, but that "there
is no reason to believe that such is the case."
I forget who is named as the author.   But,
lest any Edinburgh virtuoso should chuckle
over this example of the pot-boiler editing of
our Glasgow publishers, I have to add that

same day I saw a book of songs, with music, to which the name of a Glasgow and London publisher, Swan & Pentland, was affixed. The name of the work was *Gleadhill's Songs of the British Isles,* and in the appendix there was a biographic panegyric on the writer of this song, who the editor alleged to be John O'Keefe.

I believe it will amuse my readers to contrast the four lines that have been coupled with Burns's impassioned staccato outburst. Let them read over again the lines of Burns, and then in continuation read the following dead level smooth inanity :—

" When I showed her the ring, and implored her to marry,
    She blush'd like the dawning of morn ;
  Yes, I will ! she replied, if you'll promise, dear Harry,
    No rival shall laugh me to scorn."

This was surely composed by some Cockney coster cove, an " 'Arry " belonging to a music hall " down Whitechapel way." It raises the images in my mind of a noble staghound coupled with a bandy-legged mongrel turnspit.

7. ESTEEM FOR CHLORIS.

Ah, Chloris, since it may not be,
　　That thou of love wilt hear;
If from the lover thou maun flee,
　　Yet let the *friend* be dear.

Altho' I love my Chloris mair
　　Than ever tongue could tell;
My passion I will ne'er declare—
　　I'll say, I wish thee well.

Tho' a' my daily care thou art,
　　And a' my nightly dream,
I'll hide the struggle in my heart,
　　And say it is esteem.

Thus delicately does Burns commune with the very innermost feeling, which throughout his association with Chloris he openly proclaimed to be his sole dominant sentiment.

8. HOW LONG AND DREARY IS THE NIGHT.

Tune—"*Cauld Kail in Aberdeen.*"

How long and dreary is the night,
　　When I am frae my Dearie;
I restless lie frae e'en to morn
　　Tho' I were ne'er sae weary.

Chorus—For oh, her lanely nights are lang!
    And oh, her dreams are eerie;
  And oh, her widow'd heart is sair,
    That's absent frae her Dearie!

When I think on the lightsome days
  I spent wi' thee, my Dearie;
And now what seas between us roar—
  How can I be, but eerie?

    For oh, etc.

How slow ye move, ye heavy hours;
  The joyless day how dreary;
It wasna sae—ye glinted by
  When I was wi' my Dearie!

    For oh, etc.

In this song was sealed the poet's vow to have a song in honour of Chloris to suit the air, which Thomson disparaged as a tune for feeling and thought only suitable for lively songs, but which Burns considered capable of much expression when sung slowly. Thomson, on acknowledging it, expressed his satisfaction, and Burns says in his next letter: " I am happy that I have at last pleased you with verses to your *right hand tune* of Cauld Kail."

It may with fair reason be conjectured that

in this song Burns desired to convey to Jean Lorimer (Mrs Whelpdale) his sympathy in her probable feelings, when, in her worse than widowed condition, she returned to her parental home after the enforced desertion of her spend-thrift husband, who hastily fled under alarm at every moment of arrest and imprisonment for his reckless debts. Although his real character had been opened to her view, still she may have retained some faith in one who, only a few weeks previously, had induced her to accept him as her "partner for life," under a vow of *instant suicide* if she refused,—a vow that she, "fond fool, believed."

The song, however, is merely altered in structure from one Burns had previously contributed to Johnson's *Museum*, and in some respects is but little of an improvement on the first version, which is not encumbered with an unnecessary chorus. Scott Douglas draws attention to the improper punctuation that occurs in all the copies he has seen, and in which there is wanting the dash that should come after the word "sae" in the third stanza, and wanting which the fine meaning imparted by *glinted* is lost.

9. INCONSTANCY IN LOVE.

TUNE—"*Duncan Gray.*"

Let not Woman e'er complain
　　Of inconstancy in love;
Let not Woman e'er complain,
　　Fickle Man is apt to rove.
Look abroad thro' Nature's range,
Nature's mighty Law is change,
Ladies, would it not seem strange
　　Man should then a monster prove?

Mark the winds, and mark the skies,
　　Ocean's ebb, and ocean's flow;
Sun and moon but set to rise,
　　Round and round the seasons go.
Why then ask of silly Man
To oppose great Nature's plan?
We'll be constant while we can—
　　You can be no more, you know.

He gives Chloris the credit of this supposed complaint, but it was actually at or about the time that Burns, in his own person, illustrated the philosophy of this song. For it was at this period, in a letter to Thomson, that he alluded to Clarinda as "a *ci-devant* goddess of mine," having four months previous addressed her as

"My ever dearest Clarinda," urging that a letter
of simple .friendship was then too cold to be
attempted.   Chambers says that "it was right,
even in these poetico-Platonic affairs, to be 'off
with the old love before he was on with the
new.' . . . O, womankind! think of that
when you are addressed otherwise than in the
language of common-sense.   So lately as June
'my ever dearest,' and now (October) only a
ci-devant goddess."

10. THE LOVER'S MORNING SALUTE TO HIS
MISTRESS.

TUNE—"*Deil tak the Wars.*"

SLEEP'ST thou, or wak'st thou, fairest creature?
    Rosy morn now lifts his eye
Numbering ilka bud which Nature
    Waters wi' the tears o' joy.
    Now to the streaming fountain,
    Or up the heathy mountain,
The hart, hind, and roe, freely, wildly-wanton stray;
    In twining hazel bowers,
    Its lay the linnet pours;
    The laverock to the sky
    Ascends wi' sangs o' joy;
While the sun and thou arise to bless the day.

Phœbus, gilding the brow of morning,
    Banishes ilk darksome shade,
Nature, gladdening and adorning;
    Such to me my lovely maid.
    When frae my Chloris parted,
    Sad, cheerless, broken-hearted,
The night's gloomy shades, cloudy, dark, o'ercast
    my sky;
    But when she charms my sight,
    In pride of Beauty's light—
    When thro' my very heart
    Her burning glories dart;
'Tis then—'tis then I wake to life and joy!

In transmitting this song, with three others, to Thomson, Burns writes: "I have been out in the country, taking dinner with a friend, where I met with the lady, whom I mentioned in the second page of this odds-and-ends of a letter. As usual I got into song; and in returning home composed the following." The veracious Allan Cunningham, who touches nothing that he does not embellish *with fiction*, appends the following note to "The Lover's Morning Salute:" "Burns in a letter indicated that this song was occasioned by *sitting till the dawn at the punch bowl*, and walking past her (Chloris's) window on his way home." As usual Cunningham draws on his "boundless

I

imagination" for his facts, and rarely omits a chance
of making some disparaging allusion to habits, real
or imputed, of Burns.   In the present "lively
effort of fancy," his only text was Burns's statement
that he had been "taking dinner with a friend"
in the country. (Appendix, Note B, p. 151, and
Note C, p. 164.)

In the poet's first sketch of the song the
variation is considerable, and seems to me fairly
equal to the finished version.   But of this the
reader may judge.   Here follows the first four
lines of first stanza :

> Now thro' the leafy woods,
> And by the reeking floods,
> Wild Nature's tenants, freely, gladly stray ;
> The lintwhite in his bower
> Chants o'er the breathing flower
> The laverock, etc.

Then after the first four lines of the second stanza :

> When absent frae my Fair
> The murky shades of Care
> With starless gloom o'ercast my sullen sky ;
> But when in Beauty's light,
> She meets my ravish'd sight—
> When thro' my very heart
> Her beaming glories dart,
> 'Tis then I wake to life, to light, and joy !

II. WILT THOU BE MY DEARIE?

TUNE—"*The Sutor's Dochter.*"

WILT thou be my Dearie?
When Sorrow wrings thy gentle heart,
   O wilt thou let me cheer thee!
By the treasure of my soul,
   That's the love I bear thee;
I swear and vow that only thou
   Shall ever be my Dearie!
Only thou, I swear and vow,
   Shall ever be my Dearie!

Lassie say thou lo'es me;
Or, if thou wilt na be my ain,
   O say na thou'lt refuse me!
If it winna, canna be,
   Thou for thine may choose me,
Let me, lassie, quickly die,
   Still trusting that thou lo'es me!
Lassie let me quickly die,
   Still trusting that thou lo'es me!

Of this song, one of the best of Burns's effusions, and in which he specially prided himself, he says in a letter, March 1794:—"Do you know the much admired Highland air called 'The Sutor's Dochter.' It is a first-rate favourite of mine, and I have written what I reckon one of my best songs

to it. I will send it to you *as it was sung* with
great applause in some fashionable circles, by
Major Robertson of Lude, who was here with his
corps." Burns, in his correspondence of 1793-94,
makes frequent references to the "lobster-coated
puppies" he found visiting and hanging about
Mrs Maria Riddell's residence at that time, and
it has been surmised that she was the intended
heroine, a conjecture no doubt aided by the fact
of a grandson of the lady being possessed of the
poet's holograph copy of the song, presented to
Mrs Riddell by Burns. But I demur entirely to
this conclusion. The poem seems to me to be
perfect as a complement, and in unison with the
sentiments in (Esteem for Chloris), "Ah, Chloris,
since it may not be," written about the same
period. Almost in series, we find the link of
similar sentiment in the expression, "Wilt thou
be my Dearie, O?" which forms the refrain in the
chorus of "Lassie wi' the Lint-white Locks."
Indeed, the two songs seem written in close
continuation. But the matter is removed from
conjecture by the following fact recorded by
Scott Douglas: "At one of the Ayr festivals, on
the occasion of the poet's centenary celebrations,

Professor Traill (of Medical Jurisprudence, Edinburgh University), in giving a toast, produced a copy of this song in the bard's holograph, in which the closing stanza gives the heroineship to Jean Lorimer, thus:"

> " If it winna, canna be
>   That thou for thine may chuse me,
> Let me Jeanie, quickly die,
>   Still trusting that thou lo'es me—
> Jeanie, let me quickly die,
>   Still trusting that thou lo'es me."

Burns loved to roll this pet name of " Jeanie" like a sweet morsel under his tongue. The chorus he proposed in his first version of "O Poortith Cauld" was—

> For weel I loe my Jeanie, O,
>   I doat upon my Jeanie ;
> How happy I were she my ain,
>   Tho' I had ne'er a guinea.

On almost every suitable chance he brings in the pet name "Jeanie." In "Whistle and I'll come to ye, my lad," he had for long held that the chorus should be

> " Tho' father and mother an' a' should say no,
>   Thy Jeanie will venture wi' ye, my jo."

In "Come, let Me take Thee to My Breast,"
he says—

> "And do I hear my Jeanie own
>   That equal transports move her?"

In writing to her father, he says, "Mrs Burns
desired me yesternight to beg the favour of
Jeanie to come and partake." . . . "Jeanie
and you are all the people," etc., etc.

12. WHERE ARE THE JOYS I HAE MET?

Tune—"Saw ye my father."

WHERE are the joys I hae met in the morning,
    That danc'd to the lark's early sang?
Where is the peace that awaited my wand'ring,
    At e'enin' the wild-woods amang?

Nae mair a winding the course o' yon river,
    And marking sweet flowerets sae fair,
Nae mair I trace the light footstep o' Pleasure,
    But Sorrow, and sad-sighing Care.

Is it that Summer's forsaken our vallies,
    And grim, surly Winter is near?
No, no, the bees humming round the gay roses
    Proclaim it the pride o' the year.

Fain wad I hide what I fear to discover,
    Yet lang, lang, too well hae I known;
A' that has caused the wreck in my bosom,
    Is Jenny, fair Jenny alone.

Time cannot aid me, my griefs are immortal,
    Not Hope dare a comfort bestow:
Come then, enamour'd and fond of my anguish,
    Enjoyment I'll seek in my woe.

This fine song contrasts greatly in purity with the words of the old ballad "Saw ye my father," and is set to a delightful melody. As Mr Douglas has noted, "The Jenny [Jeanie] of this song is simply the artist's favourite model, placed with her face in shadow." The sentiment is in marked consonance with, is, indeed, but another phase of that pervading "Ah, Chloris, since it may not be," and "Wilt thou be my Dearie?"

13. BEHOLD, MY LOVE, HOW GREEN THE GROVES!

TUNE—"*My Lodging is on the Cold Ground.*"

"On my visit the other day," writes Burns, November 1794, "to my fair Chloris (that is the poetic name of the lovely goddess of my inspiration), she **suggested an idea which,** on my return from the visit, I **wrought into the** following song :"

BEHOLD, my love, how green the groves,
 The primrose banks how fair,
The balmy gales awake the flowers,
 And wave thy flowing hair.

The lav'rock shuns the palace gay,
 And o'er the cottage sings :
For Nature smiles as sweet, I ween,
 To Shepherds as to Kings.

Let minstrels sweep the skilfu' string,
 In lordly lighted ha';
The Shepherd stops his simple reed,
 Blythe, in the birken shaw.

The Princely revel may survey
 Our rustic dance wi' scorn;
But are their hearts as light as ours,
 Beneath the milk-white thorn?

The shepherd in the flowery glen;
 In shepherd's phrase will woo,
The courtier tells a finer tale,
 But is his heart as true?

These wild-wood flowers I've pu'd, to deck
 That spotless breast o' thine;
The courtier's gems may witness love,
 But 'tisna love like mine.

In his first version of this song it begins " My Chloris, mark how green the groves," and in the fourth line, the balmy gales "Wave thy *flaxen* hair."

Some months intervened between the first version, and in the interval a change had come over the poet, due to the criticisms of Thomson, who wrote, November 1794:

"Some of your Chlorises, I suppose, have flaxen hair, from your partiality for this colour—else we differ about it; for I could scarcely conceive a woman to be a beauty on reading that she had lint-white locks."

The poet had also been twitted about his use of classical names and the unsuitability of the Arcadian names of Damon, Phyllis, Sylvander, Clarinda, etc., and in a letter to Thomson, February 1796, he says:

"In my by-past songs I dislike one thing—the name of Chloris. I meant it as the fictitious name of a certain lady, but on second thoughts, it is a high incongruity to have a Greek appellation to a Scots pastoral ballad."

Referring to the change from " flaxen " to " flowing," he says:

"I have more amendments to propose. What you once mentioned of *flaxen* locks is just; they cannot enter into an elegant description of beauty. Of this again."

K

Most people will approve the giving up of
Greek names in Scottish poetry, but in yielding to
Thomson's prejudices against *flaxen* hair it must
seem to many that flaxen ringlets and lint-white
locks had long been held beautiful by Burns
himself and by his countrymen. He certainly
saw for long every beauty in Chloris, when he
described her as "the peerless queen of woman-
kind." Concerning taste there is no disputing.
To my taste Chloris's hair, a type of which is at
this moment waving around my chair on the head
of my youngest grandson, is as beautiful as the
richest ebony black, or ruddiest auburn that is to
be seen, up to the latest change in fashionable
shade, the product of the most approved hair-
washes, or balsams laid on with the best skill of
the hairdresser. The truth is that in the locks of
the "Yellow haired laddie" of popular Scottish
song—the "Yellow Locks o' Charlie," about whom
"the women are a' gane wud," and the flaxen
ringlets of the Lassie with the lint-white locks,
there is but little to discriminate—the difference
that Sambo made between his two friends Cæsar
and Pompey. They were both "bery much alike,
'specially the one on this side."

14. THE CHARMING MONTH OF MAY.

Song altered from an old English one.

It was the charming month of May,
When all the flow'rs were fresh and gay,
One morning by the break of day,
    The youthful charming Chloe—
From peaceful slumber she arose,
Girt on her mantle and her hose,
. . And o'er the flow'ry mead she goes,
    The youthful, charming Chloe.

Chorus—Lovely was she by the dawn,
    Youthful Chloe, charming Chloe,
    Tripping o'er the pearly lawn,
    The youthful, charming Chloe.

The feathered people you might see .
Perch'd all around on every tree,
In notes of sweetest melody
    They hail the charming Chloe,
Till, painting gay the eastern skies,
The glorious sun began to rise,
Outrival'd by the radiant eyes
    Of youthful, charming Chloe.

      Lovely was she, etc.

"You may think meanly of this," wrote the
poet to Thomson in transmitting it along with
the preceding song, and that which follows, "but
take a look at the bombast original, and you will

be surprised that I have made so much of it."
Burns intended his adaptation as English words
for the tune, " Dainty Davie."

A look at the "bombast original" justifies
Burns's expression, but evidently his heart was
not in the task, and he was poorly inspired
when he set to work to alter the old English
song.   And yet some have spoken highly of
this effusion, among others, I think, the Rev.
Hately Waddell.

15. LASSIE WI' THE LINT-WHITE LOCKS.

Tone—"*Rothiemurchie's Rant.*"

Chorus—Lassie wi' the lint-white locks,
            Bonie lassie, artless lassie,
        Wilt thou wi' me tent the flocks,
            Wilt thou be my Dearie, O?

Now Nature cleeds the flowery lea,
And a' is young and sweet like thee,
O wilt thou share its joys wi' me,
    And say thou'lt be my Dearie, O?

The primrose bank, the wimpling burn,
The cuckoo on the milk-white thorn,
The wanton lambs at early morn,
    Shall welcome thee, my Dearie, O.

                Lassie wi' the, etc.

And when the welcome simmer shower
Has cheer'd ilk drooping little flower,
We'll to the breathing woodbine bower,
   At sultry noon, my Dearie, O.
        Lassie wi' the, etc.

When Cynthia lights, wi' silver ray,
The weary shearer's hameward way,
Thro' yellow waving fields we'll stray,
   And talk o' love, my Dearie, O.
        Lassie wi' the, etc.

And when the howling wintry blast
Disturbs my Lassie's midnight rest,
Enclaspèd to my faithfu' breast,
   I'll comfort thee, my Dearie, O.
        Lassie wi' the, etc.

The poet in transmitting this fine effusion wrote regarding it:

"This piece has at least the merit of a regular pastoral; the vernal morn, the summer noon, the autumnal evening, and the winter night, are regularly rounded."

Scott Douglas comments on the unaccountable fact that the second stanza of this song has been omitted by Currie, Thomson, Cunningham, and Chambers, all of whom had, like himself, access to the Thomson correspondence. The verse thus omitted is in no respect inferior to any of the others. My interpretation is that the parties named had simply copied from Currie, and had not troubled to inspect the original. Currie himself omitted and altered very much at his pleasure.

"Rothiemurchie's Rant," to which the song was composed, possesses a peculiar interest as being the last melody which floated through the conscious mind of Burns. Only nine days before his death he composed a pretty little song to the air. The song of "The Lassie wi' the Lintwhite Locks" is also of peculiar interest, as furnishing the sobriquet most dear to Chloris.

16. CRAIGIEBURN WOOD.

Second Version.

Burns, in forwarding this version—May 1792, says:

"I enclose you another, and I think a better, set of 'Craigieburn Wood,' . . . to compare with the former set, as I am extremely anxious to have that song right."

Of the music, the original melody, as taken down by Burns from a country girl's singing, is generally the most approved. A few years ago a new air, by a German composer, was published by R. & J. Adams, Glasgow. Of this *infra* I have a tale to tell.

The second, or improved version runs thus :

> Sweet fa's the eve on Craigieburn,
>   And blythe awakes the morrow ;
> But a' the pride o' Spring's return
>   Can yield me nocht but sorrow.
>
> I see the flowers and spreading trees,
>   I hear the wild birds singing;
> But what a weary wight can please,
>   And Care his bosom wringing !
>
> Fain, fain would I my griefs impart,
>   Yet dare na for your anger;
> But secret love will break my heart,
>   If I conceal it langer.
>
> If thou refuse to pity me,
>   If thou shalt love another,
> When yon green leaves fade frae the tree,
>   Around my grave they'll wither.

Burns's song of Craigieburn Wood was originally composed, as has been shown, in aid of the wooing of a friend of Burns for whom he acted as poetical "black-foot."

Some years back, when on a short visit to a much-respected family of my professional *clientéle*, residing for the summer season at Moffat, we had a pleasant picnic excursion by Craigieburn to the "Grey Mare's Tail," and when passing the locality now immortalised in Burns's song I drew attention to the episode of Burns's vicarious wooing, of my reminiscence of Chloris, and of the appropriateness, from its history, of the song to furnish a delicate mode of making a declaration, always so dear to the feminine mind. It so chanced that the amiable elder daughter of my host, to whom I refer in true and not in terms of conventional eulogy, had in attendance a "hanger-on," a fine fellow, in Her Majesty's service, but imbued with the modesty so often allied with true merit. He was "blate." Of this state of things I knew nothing at the time, and on my return to town I called at R. & J. Adams, and got a copy of "Craigieburn," just set to the new air, of which the firm had purchased the copyright. It was a sweet melody, but not Scottish in character. I got the music sheet inscribed with presentation terms—what, I now forget—and had it posted to the daughter of my genial and much regarded host, now, alas, of the majority; and some weeks after, when meeting him in town, asked how "Craigieburn" had been appreciated. His

bewildered aspect brought explanation, which
broke off on his suddenly executing an extem-
porised *pas seul*, à *la* "Reel of Hulichan," while
he snapped his fingers and slapped his thighs
excitedly, bursting at last into irrepressible
laughter, for he was a man of boisterous animal
spirits, and, I add, so natural and so "straight"
in all his ways that I feel assured he was
regarded with affection as well as respect by all
his acquaintances. When he recovered sufficiently
to note my astounded and apprehensive countenance, he told me that the advent of the song
had caused some puzzlement in the family circle,
resulting in a kind acknowledgment of the piece
of music, but that the acknowledgment had not
been addressed to me, the grave old doctor,
who had never been thought of in connection,
but to the assumed donor, the modest son of
Bellona, "who only *could* be the man." The
result, as my friend explained, was an *eclair-
cissement* of the situation, in which, however, the
derivation of the song was still undeclared. But
more important. The couple, to whom might
fitly be applied "sure such a pair by nature
framed," were now engaged. My friend for a

L

time so chuckled over the incident and the fun
he would extract from it that I instinctively
fumbled in my pocket for a lancet, so as to be
in readiness to go for his jugular, in the event of
"the fit" bringing on an apoplectic one. Since
then I have occasionally seen the young pair,
now approaching middle age, happily and worthily
mated "in couple." Craigieburn is therefore to
me a reminiscence of more than Chloris.

17. I'LL AY CA' IN BY YON TOUN.

AIR—"*I'll gang nae mair to yon toun.*"

Chorus—I'll ay ca' in by yon toun,
    And by yon garden-green, again ;
I'll ay ca' in by yon toun,
    And see my bonie Jean again.

There's nane shall ken, there's nane can guess,
    What brings me back the gate again,
But she, my fairest faithfu' lass,
    And stow'nlins we sall meet again.

She'll wander by the aiken tree,
    When trystin'-time draws near again;
And when her lovely form I see,
    Oh haith ! she's doubly dear again.

I'll ay ca' in, etc.

This beautiful little song was dashed off-hand. There should be few Scottish individuals to whom it is needful to explain that "yon toun" does not mean a city, but a cluster of cottages, a clachan, or even a farm-steading, as in the old ballad of the Fox, who on his predatory excursion "had a long way to travel that night Before that he reach-éd the town, O." No doubt some of my older, or even middle-aged, readers have sang the song of the Fox, who "went out one cold winter night," in their boyhood, and have exulted in the anticipated retribution which would befall the Fox when

" Old Mistress Slipper Slapper, jumpèd out of bed,
She altered the case when she poppèd out her head ;
Get up John, get up, for the Grey Goose is dead,
And the Fox has been into the town O."

18. O WAT YE WHA'S IN YON TOWN.

Tune—"*I'll gang nae mair to yon toun.*"

Chorus—O wat ye wha's in yon town,
Ye see the e'enin' sun upon,
The dearest maid's in yon town,
That e'ening sun is shining on.

Now haply down yon gay green shaw,
  She wanders by yon spreading tree ;
How blest ye flowers that round her blaw,
  Ye catch the glances o' her e'e !
      O wat ye wha's, etc.

How blest ye birds that round her sing,
  And welcome in the blooming year ;
And doubly welcome be the Spring,
  The season to my Jeanie dear.
      O wat ye wha's, etc.

The sun blinks blythe in yon town,
  Among the broomy braes sae green ;
But my delight in yon town,
  And dearest pleasure is my Jean.
      O wat ye wha's, etc.

Without my Fair, not a' the charms
  O' Paradise could yield me joy ;
But give me Jeanie in my arms,
  And welcome Lapland's dreary sky.
      O wat ye wha's, etc.

My cave wad be a lover's bower,
  Tho' raging Winter rent the air ;
And she a lovely little flower,
  That I wad tent and shelter there.
      O wat ye wha's, etc.

O sweet is she in yon town
  The sinkin' Sun's gane down upon ;
A fairer than's in yon town
  His setting beam ne'er shone upon.
      O wat ye wha's, etc.

If angry Fate is sworn my foe,
  And suff'ring I am doom'd to bear;
I careless quit aught else below,
  But spare, O spare me Jeanie, dear!
    O wat ye wha's, etc.

This song is identified with Jean, to whose
charms it was composed, although the poet afterwards made it do duty by changing "Jeanie" to
"Lucy," and thus making the song a tributary
offering to the wife of R. A. Oswald of Auchin-
cruive, then residing in Dumfries. To complete
the adaptation, the second line of third verse was
rendered, "And on yon bonie braes of Ayr," and
the fourth line changed to "And dearest bliss
is Lucy dear." The heroineship and devotion
of the song was thus neatly transferred from one
person to another, a process by no means uncommon among poets everywhere.

19. ADDRESS TO THE WOODLARK.

Tune—"*Loch Errochside.*"

O STAY, sweet warbling woodlark, stay,
Nor quit for me the trembling spray
A hapless lover courts thy lay,
  Thy soothing, fond complaining.

Again, again that tender part,
That I may catch thy melting art;
For surely that would touch her heart
   Wha' kills me wi' disdaining.

Say, was thy little mate unkind,
And heard thee as the careless wind?
Oh, nocht but love and sorrow join'd
   Sic notes o' woe could wauken!
Thou tells o' never-ending care,
O" speechless grief, and dark despair;
For pity's sake, sweet bird, nae mair!
   Or my poor heart is broken.

This truly fine poem is an improved version
of one in the possession of the publisher of Scott
Douglas's edition. I feel tempted to give this
first version, for the first time made public by
Scott Douglas. It is entitled—

20. SONG, COMPOSED ON HEARING A BIRD SING,
   WHILE MUSING ON CHLORIS.

Sing on, sweet songster o' the brier,
Nae traitor stealthy foot is near;
O soothe a hapless lover's ear,
   And dear as life I'll prize thee.

Again, again that tender part,
That I may learn thy melting art,
For surely that would touch the heart,
   O' her that still denies me.

Oh was thy mistress, too, unkind,
And heard thee as the careless wind?
For nocht but love and sorrow joined
   Sic notes of woe could wauken.

21. YONDER POMP OF COSTLY FASHION.

AIR—"*Deil tak the Wars.*"

MARK yonder pomp of costly fashion
   Round the wealthy, titled bride:
But when compar'd with real passion,
   Poor is all that princely pride.
      Mark yonder, etc. (*four lines repeated*).

   What are the showy treasures,
   What are the noisy pleasures?
The gay, gaudy glare of vanity and art:
   The polish'd jewel's blaze
   May·draw the wond'ring gaze;
   And courtly grandeur bright
   The fancy may delight,
But never, never can come near the heart.

But did you see my dearest Chloris
   In simplicity's array;
Lovely as yonder sweet opening flower is,
   Shrinking from the gaze of day.
      But did you see, etc.

O then, the heart alarming,
And all resistless charming,
In love's delightful fetters she chains the willing
    soul !
Ambition would disown
The world's imperial crown,
Ev'n Avarice would deny,
His worshipp'd deity,
An' feel thro' every vein love's raptures roll.

22. SONG, ON CHLORIS BEING ILL.

TUNE—"*Ay Wauken, O.*"

Chorus—LONG, long the night,
    Heavy comes the morrow,
    While my soul's delight
    Is on her bed of sorrow.

Can I cease to care,
    Can I cease to languish,
While my darling Fair,
    Is on the couch of anguish !

Ev'ry hope is fled,
    Ev'ry fear is terror ;
Slumber ev'n I dread,
    Ev'ry dream is horror.

    Long, long, etc.

Hear me, Powers Divine,
   Oh, in pity hear me !
Take aught else of mine,
   But my Chloris spare me !

   Long, long, etc.

This song was written May 1795. Thomson says, in acknowledging receipt of " your pathetic address to the woodlark, and your affecting verses on Chloris's illness—every repeated perusal of these gives new delight." I believe that these sentiments will be shared by every one.

23. 'TWAS NA HER BONIE BLUE E'E.

TUNE—"*Laddie, lie near me.*"

'Twas na her bonie blue e'e was my ruin,
Fair tho' she be, that was ne'er my undoin';
'Twas the dear smile, when naebody did mind us,
'Twas the bewitching, sweet, stoun glance o' kindness,
'Twas the bewitching, sweet, stoun glance o' kindness.

Sair do I fear that to hope is denied me,
Sair do I fear that despair maun abide me,
But tho' fell Fortune should fate us to sever,
Queen shall she be in my bosom for ever,
Queen shall she be in my bosom for ever.

M

Chloris, I'm thine wi' a passion sincerest,
And thou hast plighted me love o' the dearest,
And thou'rt the angel that never can alter,
Sooner the sun in his motion would falter;
Sooner the sun in his motion would falter.

In several booksellers' "pot-boiler editions," and even in Chambers', I note that it is given "*Mary, I'm thine*," etc. The melody is a very fine one, but Burns found it difficult to get fairly "the hang of it."

24. FORLORN, MY LOVE, NO COMFORT NEAR.

Air—"*Let me in this ae night.*"

This pathetic song, put into the lips of Chloris, was sent to Thomson, May 1795. Burns asks, "How do you like the foregoing? I have written it within this hour, so much for the *speed* of my Pegasus, but what of his *bottom?*" This song is evidently designed to express the feelings of Chloris for a time after her husband's desertion.

FORLORN, my Love, no comfort near,
Far, far from thee I wander here;
Far, far from thee, the fate severe
    At which I must repine, Love.

Chorus—O wert thou, Love, but near me!
    But near, near, near me,
    How kindly thou would'st cheer me
        And mingle sighs with mine, Love!

Around me scowls a wintry sky,
Blasting each bud of hope and joy;
And shelter, shade, nor home have I,
 Save in those arms of thine, Love.

  O wert thou, etc.

Cold, alter'd friendship's cruel part,
To poison Fortune's ruthless dart—
Let me not break thy faithful heart,
 And say that fate is mine, Love.

  O wert thou, etc.

But, dreary tho' the moments fleet,
O let me think we yet shall meet;
That only ray of solace sweet
 Can on thy Chloris shine, Love!

  O wert thou, etc.

25. THINE AM I, MY CHLORIS FAIR.

TUNE—"*The Quaker's Wife.*"

THINE am I, my Chloris Fair,
 Well thou may'st discover:
Ev'ry pulse along my veins
 Proclaims the ardent lover.

To thy bosom lay my heart,
 There to throb and languish;
Tho' despair had wrung its core,
 That would heal its anguish.

Take away those rosy lips,
    Rich with balmy treasure;
Turn away those eyes of love,
    Lest I die with pleasure !

What is life when wanting Love?
    Night without a morning :
Love's the cloudless summer sky,.
    Nature gay adorning.

This song has been claimed for Clarinda, and a
version in which the second line goes, "Thine,
my lovely Nancy," is cited as evidence that
recollections of Clarinda *may* have prompted the
song; and it is stated by the editor of the
Clarinda correspondence — a statement on no
foundation — that Burns sent this effusion to
Clarinda in 1790. But Scott Douglas says there
is "not the slightest evidence that this very
successful love song was composed prior to
October 1793, when the poet sent it to Thomson"
as English words to follow his other song to the
same air, "Blythe ha'e I been on yon hill." The
"Nancy" may have been suggested as a suitable
rhyme to the third line, "Ev'ry roving fancy."
Be this as it may, Burns wrote it in August 1795,
and proposed some alterations upon the song in

which Nancy appears, and did this with a view to give Jean Lorimer the benefit of it, and wrote to Thomson in August 1795—"Did I mention to you that I wish to alter the first line of the 'Quaker's Wife' from 'Thine am I, my faithful fair' to 'Thine am I, my Chloris fair'? If you neglect the alteration, I call on all the Nine, conjointly and severally, to anathematise you."

26. (Fragment) WHY, WHY TELL THE LOVER.

TUNE—"*Caledonian Hunt's Delight.*"

WHY, why tell the lover
 Bliss he never must enjoy?
Why, why undeceive him,
 And give all his hopes the lie?
O why, while fancy, raptur'd, slumbers,
 "Chloris, Chloris" all the theme,
Why, why would'st thou, cruel—
 Wake thy lover from his dream!

On sending this "Fragment," 3rd July 1795, Burns writes:—"Such is the d——d peculiarity of rhythm of this air that I find it impossible to make another stanza to suit it."

Burns could never "get up the steam"—to venture a slang, but in this case expressive, word

—and compose to a given air until he had it played over to him or sung to him, so that he was interpenetrated with it; then he sallied out for a walk, crooning the tune and glancing around on objects that often sprang suggestive on his awakened attention; on returning home, he rocked himself on the hind legs of his chair, still crooning and jotting down expressions, until thoroughly harmonising his conceptions he would seize his pen, and, *currente calamo*, dash down the result, often with scarce a word needful for perfected completion. This fragment, however, seems to have fairly "stumped him" owing to "the peculiarity of rhythm."

27. O, THIS IS NO MY AIN LASSIE.

TUNE—"*This is no my Ain Lassie.*"

Chorus—THIS is no my ain lassie,
　　　　Fair tho' the lassie be;
　　　　Weel ken I my ain lassie,
　　　　Kind love is in her e'e.

I see a form, I see a face,
Ye weel may wi' the fairest place;
It wants to me the witching grace,
　　　The kind love that's in her e'e.

She's bonie, blooming, straight, and tall,
And lang has had my heart in thrall;
And ay it charms my very saul,
    The kind love that's in her e'e.

    This is no my ain, etc.

A thief sae pawkie is my Jean,
To steal a blink, by a' unseen;
But gleg as light are lovers' e'en,
    When kind love is in the e'e.

    This is no my ain, etc.

It may escape the courtly sparks,
It may escape the learnèd clerks;
But well the watching lover marks
    The kind love that's in her e'e.

    This is no my ain, etc.

This very fine song, with chorus, was sent to Thomson on 3rd August 1795, and for six months thereafter, with the exception of a note to the father of Chloris, already quoted, there does not seem to exist a scrap in prose or verse of the poet's writing. This, no doubt, is due to the severe and long-continued illness which set in about this time, and, with occasional intervals, afflicted him until his death in July 1796.

28. O, BONIE WAS YON ROSY BRIER.

O, BONIE was yon rosy brier,
    That blooms sae far frae haunt o' man ;
And bonie she, and ah, how dear !
    It shaded frae the e'enin' sun.

Yon rosebuds in the morning dew,
    How pure amang the leaves sae green;
But purer was the lover's vow,
    They witness'd in their shade yestreen.

All in its rude and prickly bower,
    That crimson rose, how sweet and fair ;
But love is far a sweeter flower,
    Amid life's thorny path o' care.

The pathless wild, and wimpling burn,
    Wi' Chloris in my arms be mine ;
And I the world, nor wish, nor scorn,
    Its joys and griefs alike resign.

"This," says Scott Douglas, "is apparently the last song of Burns which was inspired by the charms of Jean Lorimer, and he never excelled it in purity of sentiment and lyric beauty."

It was adapted to the air, "I wish my love was in a mire."

29. O, THAT'S THE LASSIE O' MY HEART.

Tune—"*Morag.*"

Currie took the liberty of altering the first line
to " Wha is she," and the subsequent editors have
followed suit.   But the shade of meaning is
changed.   " Wat ye " means " know ye," and
prefaces an exultant, glad inquiry, for which the
joyous response is ready.   " Oh, who do you think
is to be at the dance?" asks the eager girl, ready
to give the answer.

> O, WAT ye wha that lo'es me,
>   And has my heart a keeping?
> O, sweet is she that lo'es me,
>   As dews o' summer weeping,
>   In tears the rosebuds steeping !

> *Chorus*—O, that's the lassie o' my heart,
>   My lassie ever dearer ;
>   O, she's the queen o' womankind,
>   And ne'er a ane to peer her.

> If thou shalt meet a lassie
>   In grace and beauty charming,
> That e'en thy chosen lassie,
>   Erewhile thy breast sae warming,
>   Had ne'er sic powers alarming.

>   O, that's the lassie, etc.

N

If thou hadst heard her talking,
  (And thy attention's plighted,)
That ilka body talking,
  But her, by thee is slighted,
  And thou art all-delighted ;

    O, that's the lassie, etc.

If thou has met this Fair One,
  When frae her thou hast parted,
If every other Fair One
  But her, thou hast deserted,
  And thou art broken-hearted ;

    O, that's the lassie, etc.

This very delightful song, in four verses with chorus, is that which, it may be recollected, was sung in Burns's house by his wife at the entertainment he gave to the Edinburgh friends he so much respected, and at which he had his most respected and respectable Dumfries friends present, including Jean Lorimer and her father. The air is surpassingly sweet and peculiarly appropriate to the words, and I am amazed that it is not more frequently brought forward in chamber concerts, or " Nichts wi' Burns." (Appendix, Note E, p. 169.)

30. INSCRIPTION.

"Written on the blank leaf of a copy of the last edition of my poems,
presented to the Lady whom in so many fictitious reveries of
passion, but with the most ardent sentiments of real friendship,
I have so often sung under the name of 'Chloris.'"

'Tis Friendship's pledge, my young, fair Friend,
    Nor thou the gift refuse,
Nor with unwilling ear attend
    The moralising Muse.

Since thou, in all thy youth and charms,
    Must bid the world adieu,
(A world 'gainst Peace in constant arms,)
    To join the Friendly Few.

Since thy gay morn of life o'ercast,
    Chill came the tempest's lour,
(And ne'er Misfortune's eastern blast
    Did nip a fairer flower).

Since life's gay scenes must charm no more,
    Still much is left behind,
Still nobler wealth hast thou in store—
    The comforts of the mind!

Thine is the self-approving glow,
    Of conscious Honour's part;
And (dearest gift of Heaven below)
    Thine Friendship's truest heart.

The joys refined of Sense and Taste,
    With every Muse to rove:
And doubly were the Poet blest,
    These joys could he improve.

31. THEIR GROVES O' GREEN MYRTLE.

TUNE—"*Humours of Glen.*"

Of this song the second and fourth verses refer
to the name "Jean," and can only have been
intended for Jean Armour or Jean Lorimer, the
latter most probably, as she was at this date the
almost exclusive model.

Their groves o' sweet myrtle, let Foreign Lands reckon,
 Where bright-beaming summers exalt the perfume ;
Far dearer to me yon lone glen o' green breckan,
 Wi' the burn stealing under the lang yellow broom.
Far dearer to me are yon humble broom bowers,
 Where the blue-bell and gowan lurk, lowly, unseen ;
For there, lightly tripping, among the wild flowers,
 A-list'ning the linnet, aft wanders my Jean.

Tho' rich is the breeze in their gay, sunny vallies,
 And cauld Caledonia's blast on the wave ;
Their sweet-scented woodlands that skirt the proud palace,
 What are they?—the haunt of the Tyrant and Slave.
The slave's spicy forests and gold-bubbling fountains,
 The brave Caledonian views wi' disdain ;
He wanders as free as the winds of his mountains,
 Save Love's willing fetters—the chains o' his Jean.

This song was sent by Burns to Thomson in
May 1795, a month in which the poet was

unusually prolific in song, and specially, as throughout this summer, in verses dedicated to Chloris or Jean Lorimer. But no name was indicated, and we can only conjecture. Between May and August there are some eight or nine poems all associated with his favourite model, and none to Jean Armour. Burns was very impressionable to suggestions started by out-of-door objects in his daily walks, and it is unlikely that his wife had leisure to go tripping among wild flowers, or to listen the singing of linnets. Much more likely to be over-occupied in house affairs, cooking meals for children and servants, listening to the singing of the tea-kettle and bubbling of the potato pot. But the most conclusive reason in aid of my conjecture is the fact that the song was a favourite with my father, who spoke of it so undoubtingly as one of "Mrs Lorimer's songs,"—*i.e.*, inspired by, or dedicated to her,—that I have never questioned its derivation until I began to write out this list, since which I have diligently hunted up references, with no other than negative result. I therefore include it in the group, but, as the lawyers say, "without prejudice."

PART III.

BURNS MUCH MISUNDERSTOOD.

I AM somewhat doubtful of the effect I may have made on the minds of my readers of different classes by my rambling, gossiping reminiscence. I think it probable there will be of one type such as I am reminded of in the anecdote of a man who, after his perusal of the play of Hamlet, was asked if he had noticed anything remarkable in it. "Yes," he said, "I noticed that it was remarkably full of quotations." Of another type I am encouraged to think there may be some of the mind of Hogg, the Ettrick Shepherd, who said that he admitted a sheep's head dressed for dinner was not a very bonny dish, "but, man, there's a heap o' gude, confused feedin' aboot it."

I have had two objects in my index or group of Chloris songs—the first to show the diligence

with which Burns, as a poetic artist, availed
himself of the opportunites afforded by contact
with, and musings upon his model. There was
—but no longer is—of my boy companions, a
painter artist, of considerable note in his day, in
whose studio I had frequent opportunities of
admiring and of being interested in the manner
in which he posed his mother, sister, and brothers.
One day Meg Merrilees, Helen Macgregor, or
Lady Raleigh with her husband in the Tower;
another day a country girl waiting at the "trystin'"
place, a fisherman's young wife waiting the return
of the boats, Joan of Arc, or Maritana at a
Spanish inn buckling knightly spurs on the heels
of Don Quixote. And in like manner it may be
noted that Burns caught from his artistic intuition
the poses of emotion and of admiration inspired
by the feminine graces of his lovely young friend.
At one time he notes her mental struggles while
halting in choice. She shudders at the prospects
of "poortith cauld," and rather prefers the prospect
of rank and fashion, and her lover's peace is wrecked
as he laments that "so sweet a flower as love
depends on Fortune's shining." Then he sym-
pathises with the resolve to spurn as vilest dust

the world's wealth and grandeur, in the gratification of reciprocated affection. We see him
delightedly amusing himself, and egging on the
determination of the head-over-heels in love,
headstrong girl, who, "though father and mother
and a' should go mad," will stick to her choice.
Then he himself poses as the lover, who, beyond
the "smiling so wiling" of the bonie face of his
sweetheart, unconsciously lets out the inner secret
that surpasses all physical charms, "she says she
lo'es me best of a'."   And in his resolve to "perish
ere he'd plant in that bosom a thorn," he evinces
the nobler sentiment that shrinks from aught of
injury befalling the beloved one. The fairy sunshine glow that illumines the face of nature with
instantaneous transition, and changes the starless
gloom of his sullen sky to life, to light, and joy
occurs as she steps upon the scene. He enters into
the mind of the young peasant lad, who, gloating
on the "lint-white locks" of his artless young
companion, both alike ignorant of the deckings of
diamonds and pearls, are only conscious that the
visible world is young and sweet, and he can
think of no happier future in life than that she
will be his dearie. The human sympathies that

give interest to localities in the most primitive class of minds he touches on when he recognises that although the sun blinks "blythe" in "yon toun," his delight and greatest pleasure in yon toun is "my Jean." And keenly and touchingly he evinces his sympathies with all animated creatures, who can love and enjoy, he discloses in his address to the songster on the brier, while musing on Chloris. His sympathy for "a beloved" while she is on the couch of anguish makes his nights long and his days clouded in the morrow. How quickly he catches the contrast between the mere beauty of the "bonie blue e'e" that could ruin—that is, utterly conquer; but beyond and above that charm sees the dear smile, when naebody did mind us. He sees the bewitching, sweet, stolen glance o' kindness. But why need I turn in kaleidoscopic fashion the varied illustrations which the songs inspired by Chloris show of the humanity of Burns's nature, that humanity, which far and away beyond the admiration with which we regard a Shakespeare, Pope, Homer, or Dante, makes Burns a brother, a near relation— a name that is a reality as an object of personal affection.

O ,

It is with the object of indicating how much of good the influence of Chloris inspired—innocently and legitimately inspired; but there is another point of view that I would fain have my readers look at with my eyes. It is a view in which Burns always appears to me on an elevated pedestal. The view I take of his manly, chivalrous bearing towards Chloris when bleeding under the cruel wound to her self-esteem in the desertion of her worthless scamp of a husband, the idol of her young inexperience, and when under the humiliating ordeal of return among her friends of but yesterday she was subject to, we know not what, of gecks and scorns of her neighbours and others, so lately her rivals. It was then that Burns came boldly forward and did what as a man it seemed open for him to do. He soothed her injured pride, bleeding from the incurable wound inflicted by her despicable husband, and by his attentions and such marks of regard *as became him to bestow*, he aided her in a crisis of mental struggle that threatened her with utter despair. To his eyes, as he widely and *publicly* proclaimed, she was an object of pity, of admiration, and of respect. Of world's wealth he had none to bestow, but he was now known as a man of mind—of independent mind—quick to assert his prerogative anywhere and everywhere—prompt to act strongly—

> "For the cause that lacks assistance,
> For the wrong that needs resistance,
> For the future, in the distance,
> And the good that he could do."

And he was feared because of his known strength —a dangerous man to offend, "for he could hing up an offender in a sang like a potato bogle." He was known to have a keen and wide knowledge of womankind, and well qualified to discriminate. He was also known as the anxious head of a young family, and a careful father, despite what otherwise, or even still, may be thought by *very ignorant* individuals of the unco guid and rigidly righteous kind. He could not, he considered, better the service of a true friend than by his *open, manly discrimination*, and by his kind *sympathy*—the neighbourly sympathy that can ease us (except under that "hell o' a' diseases," the toothache), and he thus sustained the afflicted mind of Jean Lorimer for several years.' He never missed an opportunity of cherishing her "self-approving glow of conscious honour," and in so doing added to the "chief joys" that yet remained to a blighted life. His last lines in his last address to her are—

> "And doubly were the Poet blest,
> These joys could he improve."

He never, so far as known, spoke or wrote a word concerning her that could lessen her self-esteem throughout the years of their association, and his bearing was always that of almost fatherly tenderness. Of this feeling he gives proof and touching expression to in the inscription I have quoted, written in a blank leaf of a volume of his poems, presented 3rd August 1795. It was from the point of view I now indicate, and because of the comfort that Burns's association with, and references to, his young friend did impart, that my father implanted early in my mind the conviction that *Burns was a man much misunderstood,* just as he assured me that Chloris had been much misunderstood. It is only where such misunderstanding lingers that there can be a disposition to class Chloris among the "red flower loves" of Burns, a class in which Clarinda must be included. Clarinda was indeed a most fascinating woman, much more talented, but not a Jean Lorimer. In every respect the feeling of Burns towards Clarinda was in marked contrast to that evinced to "Jeanie."

Burns's acquaintanceship of some four months with Clarinda in Edinburgh was, in contrast, practically a tournament of literary calisthenics, engaged in by Burns *pour passes le temps* (for "he had nothing else to do," as he admitted), but undoubtedly by Clarinda *a l'outrance;* and when he made escape from the Circe in March 1791, he wrote from Glasgow to a friend, "*These eight days I have been positively crazed.*" During the delirious nightmare of the everyday letter, reply, explanation, and rejoinder, which seemingly formed the entire occupation of the bewitched couple, Burns wrote all kinds of stuff that might, could, would, or should be—or should *not* be—but at no time did he forget himself with Chloris, or address her in such lines as "O May, thy morn was ne'er sae sweet as the mirk nicht o' December," the date of his final parting with Clarinda—innocent, there is little doubt—but, even on the surface, somewhat warmly coloured. Burns's passion

for Chloris was altogether a "white flower
love." (Appendix, Note A, p. 150.)

"The case," says Chambers, "was *literally* as he himself
states it. Fascinated by the beauty of this young creature
(Chloris), he erected her as the goddess of his inspiration,
at the same time that *respect for her intelligence and pity
for her misfortunes* were sufficient, supposing the absence
of other restraints, to debar all unholier thoughts."

It will be recollected that, when speaking of
the writings of Burns, placed in my hands sixty-
four years ago by Chloris, I alluded to the only
specimen remaining accessible to me—viz., "The
Song of Death." On the same sheet of manuscript the poet had began to compose, or to copy,
but had written only one line—"O turn again,
thou fair Rabina"—when, by a sudden, hasty
movement, seemingly of a finger, the line was
smeared and half obliterated, while the ink was
still wet. The intended purpose had been abandoned—the sheet turned other edge up, and "The
Song of Death" begun and completed. This
line, "O turn again, thou fair Rabina," has
furnished a peg on which I purpose to hang
some critical comments *apropos* of imperfect
versions and erroneous records of the works of
Burns. (Appendix, Note F, p. 173.)

It has always been evident that the fine song " Turn again, thou fair Eliza" is only a variation of one to " The fair Rabina," and further believed that Chambers's history of the poem was the correct one. It has only of late become known that his account is altogether erroneous—very interesting, but not true. He says,—

> " Burns composed this song to a Highland air which he found in Macdonald's collection. In the original manuscript the name of the heroine is Rabina, which he is understood to have afterwards changed to Eliza *for reasons of taste*. Mr Stenhouse relates that the verses were designed to embody the passion of a Mr Hunter, a friend of the poet, towards a Rabina of real life, who, it would appear, was loved in vain, for the lover went to the West Indies, and there died soon after his arrival."

But with a plain tale Scott Douglas puts down this very circumstantial detail. The true version is, as usual, "stranger than fiction." According to Mr Douglas,

> " This elegant lyric seems to have been composed in fulfilment of a promise made by the author to Mr James Johnson, the engraver and publisher of the *Musical Museum*. In a letter to him dated 15th November 1788, after expressing himself in a highly complimentary strain regarding that publication, he thus concludes :—' Have you never a fair goddess that leads you a wild-goose chase of amorous devotion? Let me know a few of her qualities, such as whether

she be rather black or fair, plump or thin, short or tall, etc., etc., and choose your air, and I shall task my muse to celebrate her.'"

Mr Douglas reminds us that Burns made a similiar offer to Thomson, suggesting verses arranged in the alternate way of a lover and his mistress chanting together in dialogue form. Thomson, in reply, stated that his name being "Geordie," and his wife's "Katie," they were too burlesque for the suggested poem.

"We are not certain," says Mr Douglas, "that Johnson was a married man at that date. His wife, whose name was Charlotte Grant, survived her husband twenty years; but in the meantime he selected the name 'Rabina' for the honour of being thus celebrated by Burns. Accordingly we find in the Hastie collection of the poet's manuscripts in the British Museum two versions of the song in the text, one of which is addressed to 'Thou fair Rabina,' and another to *Eliza*, as being deemed more euphonious for vocalisation."

Below the first of these, Burns has thus written:

"So much for your Rabina! How do you like the verses? I assure you I have tasked my muse to the top of her performing."

"The lyric," says Mr Douglas, "is a very successful one; and Burns rarely, if ever, surpassed the closing eight lines, which roll on with accumulating force till a climax of rapture is attained. We wonder that the song has not hitherto commanded the efforts of some musical composer to fit it with worthy melody. The two airs given in the *Museum*—both Gaelic—are 'most base bad.'"

In this matter Chambers's error is very venial, arising, no doubt, from misinformation, and in no way affecting the sentiment of the author or the value of the poem.

It is amusing to learn that this question, so conclusively settled by Scott Douglas, had yet another version, contributed by Allan Cunningham, who "*nullum quod tetigit, non ornavit,*" and who found in the uncommon name Rabina, an opportunity for the exercise of that "boundless imagination" that so impressed his friend Hogg, the Ettrick Shepherd. For Cunningham records, with all the *vraisemblance* of one who personally knows all about it, and who—from the circumstantiality of his details might be conjectured as in the habit of taking tea and supper with the personages referred to,—that "the name of the heroine was *at first* Rabina; but Johnson the publisher, *alarmed* at admitting *something new into verse,* caused Eliza to be substituted; which was *a positive fraud*"—continues honest Allan, always prompt in the expression of "noble sentiments"

—"for Rabina was *a real lady*, and *a lovely one*, and Eliza one of air." As Hogg says, when honest Allan once began, -"no one could say at what he would stop." (Appendix, Note B, p. 151, Note C, p. 164, and Note F. p. 173.)

But, continuing my reference to this special sheet of Burns's manuscript, I am led to notice another kind of error for which some editors are fairly responsible. Before doing so I think it well to copy the poem referred to in full, so that the reader may more readily follow me beyond the line of the "fair Rabina." The poem in itself is well worthy of frequent reproduction because of its intrinsic merit, being, in the opinion of Thomas Campbell, one of the most brilliant effusions of the poet. (Appendix, Note G, p. 174.) It has, indeed, been extolled in very high terms. Dr Currie struck the first note of admiration regarding it. It was about the close of 1791, and before the enthusiasm generated by the progress of the French Revolution had waned into terror and disgust, that Burns brought out this hymn, worthy of the Greek muse when Greece was most conspicuous for genius and valour. Dr Currie says in a footnote, "this noble poem seems more calculated to invigorate the spirit of defence in a season of real and pressing danger than any other production of modern times." The reader will note some words which I give in italics for the purpose of comment.

THE SONG OF DEATH.

Farewell, thou fair day; thou green earth; and ye skies,
    Now gay with the *broad*-setting sun !
Farewell, loves and friendships, ye dear, tender ties !
    Our race of existence is run.

Thou grim king of terrors, thou life's gloomy foe,
    Go frighten the coward and slave,
Go, teach them to tremble, fell tyrant ! but know,
    No terrors hast thou to the Brave.

Thou strik'st the *dull* peasant, he sinks in the dark,
    Nor saves e'en the wreck of a name ;
Thou strik'st the young hero, a glorious mark !
    He falls in the blaze of his fame.

In the field of proud Honor, our swords in our hands,
    Our king and our country to save,
While victory shines on life's last ebbing sands,
    O ! who would not *die* with the Brave !

In the foregoing the text is given literally, and yet, by the tampering of some editors, the meaning of the author is perverted to suit the critical tastes of these editors. With the exception of two words, no attempt was made by Burns himself to improve it. These words are the substitution of *broad* for bright in the second line, and of *die* for rest in the last line, and all editors who have considered these amendments have approved. But tastes differ, for Craibe Angus, when examining my manuscript with keen eye, pointed to the word broad, observing that in another copy, also in Burns's handwriting, the word *bright* is used instead, and that it seemed somewhat doubtful which was the preferable word. Regarding my manuscript, he considered it a finely characteristic example, and interesting, irrespective of the line to fair Rabina, or to the endorsement of the poem in the handwriting of Jean Lorimer on the back, adding, with a jocund twinkle of his eye, that he would "almost go to jail for its possession."

It is unlikely that any of my Burns readers require to be told that Craibe Angus is generally regarded as the most authoritative, as he is the most *experienced* expert in all that relates to the authentication of Burns documents, and that he has well merited this high appreciation because of the share he had in unmasking the alleged traffic in forgeries of " Burns manuscripts" so recently brought before the public in the Edinburgh Law Courts. Regarding the use of the word *broad*, instead of *bright*, it seems to me there should be little dubiety. The scene is a battlefield, strewed with dead and dying, the latter gazing on the broad *setting* orb that for the last time, to their eyes, is illuminating a landscape still gay, although fading. Here the *broad* disc is characteristically indicative of *a setting* sun. But to have the word *bright* following upon gay seems to me tautological, and can contribute nothing to the sentiment of a setting, vanishing sun "with disc like battle target red." I think that most persons will approve the word *broad*, which Burns finally selected.

But a different consideration must be given to the word *dull*, which I have underlined, and which has been tampered with by some pot-boiler editors, who have substituted the word *poor*, and their version is "the *poor* peasant"—a mighty difference in meaning. For "dull" has no reference to *position in life* or to the *possession of wealth;* it means *doltish,* wanting in sensibility,

in keenness of perception. Surely of all men
Burns is the last liable to the reproach of
slighting his fellow-man for lack of riches, or
because of humble social position. Himself poor,
also a peasant, he yet proclaimed in words that
will ring while the world endures, that "A man's
a man" whether he dines on homely fare or wears
hodden gray—that a lord, decked with stars and
ribbons, may be but a fool, and that "An honest
man, *though e'er so poor*, is king o' men for a'
that." The word "poor," to my thinking, quite
destroys the meaning of Burns, and it is only a
dull corrector of the press, not to speak of an
editor, who can fail to see this. The young hero
who in his latest moments apostrophises the
"grim king of terrors" may be merely *a peasant*
as well as *a poor* one—as the first of the notable
race of Douglas was—but he is still a hero,
having a soul apart from that of the dull clod-
hopper, and when prone on the proud field of
honour, but surrounded with kindred spirits, he,
for king and country, meets death in a rapture
of welcome.

Such mutilations of the poet's ideas are by no
means confined to the cheap *réchauffés* of Burns.

Very recently, in a shop in Buchanan Street, Glasgow, there was placed in my hands by the salesman a portly cabinet edition, in which, as one of the latest issued, I wished to ascertain if some poems recently recovered, such as the song of "The Thorn," had yet found admission to their legitimate preserve. It was an elegantly got-up volume, faultless in respect to binding, paper, and typography. But because of a perplexing, literally unusable, index, I failed in my search, as did also the intelligent bookseller, who came to my aid. He expressed surprise, as the book was from a firm that claimed special credit for the perfection of its goods. The only alternative was to search page by page, and in doing a little in this way I stumbled on "The Song of Death." But, as in a number of plebeian shilling malformations, "the poor peasant" stared in my face, and I returned the volume, glancing at the title-page for identification. It bore to be issued from the Oxford University Press, and had the single word "Frowde" as publisher, much as the names of Buccleuch, Norfolk, or Argyll are held sufficient evidence of unquestionable rank and position. Singularly enough, I have since learned

—if I understand aright—that it is only the title-
page and the binding that is the product of the
Oxford University Press—the entire letterpress
being some pot-boiler printer's speculation, taken
over and issued under cover of a more aristocratic
firm, and that reams of printed matter so got up
are hawked about by printers' "drummers" and
disposed of among so-called publishing booksellers, who supply their name and a title-page
only. I saw no name of editor, or evidence of
editing, in this edition, but it was, I repeat, a
very handsomely got-up bookseller's pot-boiler,
and the only references or claims to the confidence of the public were to be found in
the words "Frowde" and "Oxford University
Press." (Appendix, Note H, p. 178.)

There is, however, no difficulty in access to
fairly usable editions of Burns, but a choice
must be made, for, as shown, it is not sufficient
that the volume is handsomely got up, or that
it bears the name of a respectable printer or
publisher. As a rule, those are to be avoided
termed "Cabinet" editions, which are usually
abridgments, selections, etc., and also too often
wanting in the name of some notable literary

man, which *quantum valeat* is a warranty that a supervision has been exercised, other than that of the printer's type-setting-room, other than the almost mechanical one of pointing commas, periods, and paragraphs. As a good example of these condensed editions, indeed one of the best, and also cheapest, I may cite that of Alexander Smith (Globe edition. Macmillan, publisher), in which it is evident that some intelligent consideration has been given to ensure that the text is in accordance with the most approved versions; and some of them, as that of Alexander Smith, are accompanied with a fairly epitomised biographical sketch of Burns, together with a critical commentary on the extent, variety, and influence of his poetical works. But on the whole these condensed, abridged selections vary little, save in the degree in which they may have a few poems not included in other editions of the class; or it may be illustrated by a few anecdotes, notes, glossary, or other extras, but practically they are mere reproductions— "Cauld kail-het again."

But of the professedly complete editions (Appendix, Note B, p. 151), none are complete

Q

which do not include the correspondence of Burns,
without which no reader can hope to know
Burns, *just as he was.*   Indeed, the letters of
Burns furnish an amount of reading matter,
interesting, instructive, and actually fascinating, in no degree second to the poems, and
not conceivable by one who has hitherto disregarded this, the only available source *now*
through which can be formed a true conception
of this remarkable Scotsman.   It is universally
conceded that no more reliable, and therefore
valuable, biography exists than that of Boswell's
Life of Johnson.   The everyday walk and
conversation of his hero is recorded by Boswell
with a conscientious diligence that photographed
his conversations on the spot, and that stimulated
him often to traverse London in order to fix a
date or the verity of a word or expression, and
thus we have Johnson in his morning, noon,
and night aspect, as no other man has been
recorded.   Next to these lip utterances, we may
place the prompt, spontaneous records of a man
whose almost every thought, as it was conceived,
was recorded, for the pen was ready in Burns's
hand with opportunity; and it was because of

this peculiarity, and with Boswell's *Johnson* in his mind, that Dr Currie so engaged the attention of the public by committing to the press about one hundred and twenty letters of Burns—"the recent and unpremeditated effusions of a man of genius." The result has been that the public verdict in their favour is nearly as strong as its estimation of his poetry. "From the correspondence," says Scott Douglas, "as surely as from the verse of Burns proceeds a vivid reflex of the writer's mind and character; and scarcely is it a figure of speech to rank both of these as a portion of his autobiography." It is by no means because of temptation to stretch my tether beyond the ring-fence of my reminiscences, or of a desire to browse in fields and pastures new, that I venture to comment on some of the editions of Burns. It is because I feel it needful for one object I had in prominent view when I took pen in hand to place my reminiscences and conception of Chloris before readers and students of Burns. That object was to ensure, as well as I could, that she should be looked at all round with the aid of such side-lights as are shown by biographers of Burns, by his poems, and such as are reflected *ab intra* through Burns's letters, and in especial, it was with my father's expressions in my mind, that Chloris was a woman much misunderstood, as well as her true friend Burns. (Appendix, Note J, p. 179.)

And this consideration leads me to an *apropos* reminiscence among the many recollections that crowd the road I am traversing, and on which at every standpoint as I pause—

> " Hills peep o'er hills, and seem to rise
> As a look is backward cast
> To some well-remembered spot that lies
> In the sunshine of the past."

At the banquet in the City Hall, Glasgow, on the occasion of the centenary celebration of 1859, the late Dr Norman Macleod was one of the platform speakers, and he created a strong sensation. He responded to the toast of " The Scottish Clergy," and did so in a speech second to none in eloquence or in the generous fervour with which he appreciated all that could be and that was claimed for Burns, showing that he had welded Scottish hearts throughout the world in a common bond of brotherhood—consolidated a fabric of nationality and patriotism distinctively

Scottish, and elevated the tone and delicacy of feeling of the Scottish people above that prevailing before his day. Up till this point Dr Macleod carried with him the enthusiastic approval of his vast auditory. *But*, he continued, but how could he as a clergyman forget to note, to lament, and to condemn, much for which Burns was reprehensible? He was not called upon to pass judgment on Burns as a man, but only as a writer, and it was with the deepest sorrow, but from his heart, he said there were poems written by Burns which merited the severest condemnation; that for Burns's own sake, and that of those who loved him most, would God they were never written, never printed and never read. The uproar caused by this bold traversing of the hitherto unbroken sentiment of the assembly was indescribably great; nearly the entire meeting, numbering about 1200 individuals, rose to their feet, and the hissing and hooting became really tremendous, and vain efforts were made by the chairman (Sir A. Alison) and the influential platform guests to procure for the speaker a further hearing. Some shouted "What of the Bible?" others, "What about Shakespeare?"

At the table adjoining mine a gentleman, who,
I think, must have been a coal agent, cried out
several times, "He just means they should
be *screened*"—that being the technical expression
that indicates the trade process of separating
dross from coal. Dr Macleod evidently felt
keenly the perfect whirlwind of censorious uproar
directed against him, and the sight of the sea
of angry faces, for his own face became turgid,
as I noted sitting within six yards, and he several
times shouted, "You mistake me. Hear me."
At length, under the supplicating gestures of
the chairman and platform speakers, the storm
subsided, and Dr Macleod in a momentary
interval succeeded in adding that he would
rejoice to see, as a result of these festivals
in honour of Burns, a centenary edition of
his poems *from which everything was excluded
that a father could not read aloud to his family
circle, or could leave open in his absence to be
read by his sons and daughters.* "In such
case he would rejoice in the hope that there
would be a copy of Burns in every dwelling in
Scotland, from the mansion to the lowliest
cottage."

In this sentiment I have never since ceased to share. It has nevertheless many opponents, and, as Sir Roger de Coverley observed, "much may be said on both sides." There are among the millions of Burns votaries very many who will not have their literary food cut and spooned out for them. With true Protestant feeling, they *will* "judge for themselves," will look suspiciously distrustful at all Bowdlerised, expurgated editions, and crave the genuine, unadulterated early Kilmarnock editions, not, as I have had frequent evidence, because of possible gratification of what is "in," but of the most jealous apprehension of what may be kept "out." As the young lady remarked to her parents, who were denying her the enjoyment of a public ball because of the many perils which in their day they had "too well seen all the folly of," "But I want to see all the folly of it, too," she plaintively pleaded. And therefore true students of Burns wish to judge for themselves of Burns's faults, his morality, and of the backslidings so long and so persistently urged, too frequently by individuals who could not themselves stand alongside him before a well-illuminated mirror;

they crave to see Burns *just as he was*, "in all the naked majesty of man," and will have "the text, the whole text, and nothing but the text."

Tempora mutantur, nos et mutamur in illis, and it is truly wonderful how "use doth breed a habit in a man," as illustrated in everyday experience. Lady Brassey and Ida Pfeiffer, without a blush or a fan, record their journeyings among the varied people who run up no bills with tailors and dressmakers. We see, and do not shrug as we see, the delicately-brought-up young ladies and gentlemen who at theatre and opera sit side by side and gaze unabashed at troops of female dancers who, attired in a pair of dancing shoes, and a muslin frill round the waist, frisk, pirouette, and ta-ra-ra within a few yards. In our drawing-rooms, and at our Court presentations, how usual it is for ladies to be seen on whom the extreme efforts of ingenuity have been expended, so that they may seem to be clothed while decked with little more than a train or skirt, and such other articles of toilette attached to the skirt as seem to conceal what they wish to reveal. "Oh, go away, you horrid man!" here exclaims Mrs Grundy. "If you come an inch nearer, I'll scream!" So I pause.

There is much, indeed, to be said in behalf of the earnest student of Burns who loves not wisely but too well, and collects early editions —*par excellence, the* Kilmarnock editions. It is too often the eye that sees in which the real indelicacy exists. It has been remarked by a keen moralist that individuals of extreme nicety are often individuals of nasty ideas. "Fie, for shame!" said a lady, catching up her young progeny, who was indecorously sprawling on the carpet. "Do not mind, madam," said Dean Swift; "it is all in the way of innocence." It's human nature, says the Burns opponent of expurgation, as he contends that the native delicacy of a Florence Nightingale or of her disciple, the modern professional nurse, is not to be belittled before a modern ball-room or Court lady. He points to the habits of the army, which, as Uncle Toby affirms, "swore terribly in Flanders," and continued to swear through last century into this, as evidenced in the every utterance of "the Great Duke" and of Admiral Napier, in the sympathetic and cordial

R

imitation of army and naval officers, the peerage,
the squirearchy, and the judicial bench, up till
and after Burns's day, who, poor man, never came
within measurable distance of the upper crust
of British society in coarseness and indelicacy of
expression. (Appendix, Note K, p. 179.) But that
is no palliation in the judgment of the implacable
censors of Burns, and I fear too often for
reasons other than those professed.   For there
are "classes and masses," and "that which in
the captain's but a *choleric word*, is in the soldier
flat blasphemy."

How true it is that familiarity breeds contempt
—that is, indifference.

> " Vice is a monster of so frightful mien,
>   As to be hated needs but to be seen ;
>   Yet seen too oft, familiar with her face,
>   We first endure, then pity, *then embrace.*"

"I maun admit," said a decent old Scotch lady,
"that my nephew *does* swear maist awfu', but
—but, ye ken, it's whyles a great set-aff to conversation."   Many of my readers will remember
the doings of the Fudge Family in Paris, so
wittily narrated by Thomas Moore.   They may
recall one adventure of Miss Biddy, where in a

picnic she got into a romantic flirtation with a
prince *en mufti*, or "*at least* a colonel," of
pronounced political views, and with a fine taste
for *shades of colour* in costumes, who suddenly
asked Miss Biddy, "Who made her gown?"
But here Miss Biddy must speak for herself in
her confidential letter to a bosom friend at
home in Kilkenny:

> " I stammered out something—nay, even half named,
> The *legitimate* sempstress, when loud, he exclaimed,
> ' Yes, yes, by the stitching, 'tis plain to be seen
> It was made by that Bourbonite b——h, VICTORINE.'
> What a word for a HERO!—but heroes *will* err,
> And I thought, dear, I'd tell you things *just* as they are;
> Besides, though the word on good manners intrench,
> I assure you, 'tis not *half* so shocking in French."

I am not so sure of this, but it is evident that
Miss Biddy was quite as ready to palliate, even
after she had translated into vernacular for the
benefit of her correspondent, the objectionable
word—to palliate while her hero, in her belief,
was a prince or "at least a colonel," but not
when the illusion was past,

> " And the hero she worshipp'd—vile, treacherous thing,
> Had turned out but a low linen draper at last ! "

I think, although pitying poor Miss Biddy, that
even the *chien femelle* that I assume was the

pseudo prince's expletive *should* have shocked
her quite as much as when not translated into
English, and I think that my readers, in this
age of missing word competitions, have had
no difficulty in guessing the word that I have
so delicately indicated by a printer's dash, ——;
and I think that words which so familiarly
garnish the conversation printed and spoken by
girls, women, and men in France and in French
literature, are quite as shocking in French as
in English ; and it grates on my ears and rasps
my eyes to see *Bon Dieu, Mon Dieu*, etc., etc.,
"familiar as household words," a name at which
every head should bow.   Therefore, while making
every allowance reasonably claimable, I am far
from tolerating the *naturalistic* proclivities of
fanatic Burnsites, who hold that what is *only
natural* is tolerable.   Substantially their motto
is : *Omne verum utile dictu*—and because it is
true it may therefore be uttered.

But there are many things which, however
natural, and neither *sinful* nor *criminal*, may
yet be *shameful*, and although ultra-fastidious-
ness is to be deprecated, there are sights and
sounds to which our attention should not be

compelled in printed books or in conversation. No doubt we may close our eyes and ears, as Yankee ladies are said to do when allusion is made to the *legs* of any person, animal, or thing, and open them again when these articles are *properly* referred to as "lower limbs" (the lower limbs of pianos are alleged to be occasionally draped in muslin "pantlets"). And no doubt it is blamable not to wink considerately or to *look* too closely at what we often unavoidably *see*, and no doubt what the eye sees the heart too aptly longs for, as does that of the over-head-and-ears lover in a ball-room, whose

> "Charmed eye o'er fifty fair ones roves,
> He *sees* them all, but *looks* at her he loves."

"Doctor," said an old lady to Dr Johnson, "why did you put so many bad words in your Dictionary?" "So, madam," said the Doctor, "you have been looking for them."

But, all said and admitted that can be said and admitted for enthusiastic votaries of Burns, there remains the fact that our very best, in as far as being *the most complete*, editions of the poet's work contain much that *should never be printed and never be read* save for and by *literary*

pathologists; and there is assuredly open to an
enterprising publisher a field quite apart from
that where Mrs Bowdler or her congeners of
the "prunes-and-prism" Euphemists—the unco'
guid and rigidly punctilious—may ruminate in
maiden meditation, and with no need of walking
circumspectly to avoid the snares and pitfalls of
the early editions; and the ghoulish pathologists
may continue to enjoy undisturbed seclusion
within the walls of their own dissecting-room and
mortuary.   At the same time, I as strongly as
any resent any forgeries through alterations, sub-
stitutions (Appendix, Note B, p. 151), or softening
down through printer's dashes and isolated letters
any words or sentences which plainly reveal what
they seem to conceal, for heroes *will* err, and
occasional expletives *are* characteristic and may
be blotted from the record of everyday memory,
as the oath of Uncle Toby was blotted out by
the tear of the recording angel because of "the
cause."

I can cite no better exponent of my meaning
than Burns himself regarding what, in my opinion,
is clearly a *desideratum* among the innumerably
varied editions of Burns. Burns himself is the

best interpreter of his own wishes while in that state of mind that results from calm consideration and conclusive judgment. What he desired and was satisfied with should please his devoted admirers. He should be taken at his deliberate word, and that word I will immediately make forthcoming. Still, I fear that there will remain some—a fast diminishing number, I trust—who are more Burns, in their conception, than he himself was, and who will continue to crave for and to collect the old Kilmarnock editions and reprints—the text, the whole text, and nothing but the text, their last words. In this class it is with regret that I include Scott Douglas, the editor of by far the most complete, the most reliable, the most suitable for the uses of the earnest student of Burns. For Scott Douglas was an editor of a thousand. He was a veritable literary sleuth-hound in tracking down a date, fact, or incident when he once got "on the scent." In a private letter I am told by one who had the best means of knowing him, "from within his inmost centre to his outmost skin," that "no more conscientious editor ever passed book through his hands—and his edition of Burns

(1891) was the result of a life's study and labours."
Conscientiousness is good, but we may have too
much of a good thing. Mr Douglas in this
creditable characteristic reminds me of a similarly
honest-minded old Scotch carrier who had in
charge to deliver "a pock o' sweeties" at the
general dealer's store of a country village. The
cording of the bag had given way, and the
sweeties got strewn all over the floor of the van,
mixed up with straw, bits of string, paper, dust,
and all other *débris* of the miscellaneous cargo.
The conscientious carrier—call him Scott Douglas
—asked the goodwife of the store to lend him a
"brod" or tray, with which in one hand, and
wielding his Tam o' Shanter "bannet" in the
other, he "dadded," and swept, and dusted out
of every corner, chink, and crevice the last comfit,
together with all the undesirable accompaniments
into the tray, and with "the self-approving glow
of conscious honour" laid the tray upon the
counter. "Here they are, missis; ye hae them
a' for me," he said. Mr Douglas, conscientiously
scrupulous in delivering to his Burns readers *all
he can*, withholds *nothing*. A little way back, when
I narrated the history and gave my readers the

first version of Burns's song of "Craigieburn Wood," I stated that Thomson wrote Burns to the effect that the chorus he proposed was quite out of the question, and could not possibly be given in company where ladies were present. And Mr Stephen Clarke, the musical editor of *Johnson's Museum*, wrote Thomson saying to never trouble himself about the chorus, for the man who would attempt to sing it to such a song should have his throat cut to prevent his singing it again. Burns backed out of blame, assuring Thomson that the chorus *was* none of his work, and was only the doggerel chorus he had picked up along with the tune. But Scott Douglas, irreconcilably conscientious, says in a foot-note with most amusing *naïveté*, "We rather like the chorus;" and we can imagine him humming it over with gloating appreciation. And so, no doubt, there will be those who will nuzzle and mumble and hold carnival over the nasty early Kilmarnock editions. *Requiescunt in pace.*

And yet of all editions, that of Scott Douglas is by far the one to be preferred, as well by enthusiastic Burns students as by those who seek a book for the family circle, because *it supplies a*

S

basis and wealth of material nowhere else accessible.
Of course, I say this "*with qualification.*" A few
words will show wherein it is pre-eminently
distinguished from all its predecessors, and is
unlikely to be overtaken or superseded by any
which will follow. Of *professedly* complete editions
of Burns, it is needful to refer only to four—those
of Currie, Cunningham, Chambers, and Scott
Douglas. The first, in above twenty editions,
dates from 1800 to 1835, all very incomplete,
much tampered with, and quite out of date. The
second, dating in some half-dozen reprints from
1834 to about 1850—none complete or in any
way to be relied upon, and also long out of
date. The third, dating 1850 and reprinted 1857,
honest and able, a charming edition, and my
special favourite up till its date, but subject to
much correction because of inaccuracies, and out
of date because not containing much material
since available. The fourth, that of Scott
Douglas, an edition limited to 500 signed
copies, of which, it is probable, there are now
few obtainable, is thoroughly up to date, and
a perfect mine of the poet's works in prose
and verse.

It is interesting to contrast the material which time and the labours of these editors have enabled them to pile before the readers and students of Burns. Currie gives in part, selections, and abbreviations about 120 letters, somewhat increased in the later editions. Cunningham boasts, as he generally was inclined to do, that he presents 150 above the number of Currie—in all a total of 327 letters, but only partially quoted in numerous instances; in that respect resembling his predecessor. Chambers gives, more or less fully, a total of 387 letters, and in corresponding ratio 286 poems; while Scott Douglas gives unmutilated no less than 534 letters, correspondence, and other productions, of which a considerable portion, say about 130, are in part or in whole published for the first time. Of poems, Scott Douglas gives 650, and all his literary material is corrected up to Burns's latest amendments or corrections, is verified by reliable references, and arranged chronologically throughout, forming, in its entirety, the most compendious memorial hitherto printed, alike of the wonderful genius of our national bard, and the most creditable example of diligent industry furnished by any of his commentators.

To many these facts will be matter of surprise, as also of interest, not alone respecting the prose matter that has been gradually unearthed, but because of the number of poems which were less likely to have remained in obscurity. The explanation regarding the latter is, however, simple enough. Burns, in common with other poets, did not in every case amend and polish his verses before entrusting copies to his friends. On the contrary, under the pressure of his own riper judgment, or in deference to friendly criticism, he amended, altered, and re-wrote entirely improved versions. Thus, of "Ye Banks and Braes" there were three variations, of "Craigieburn Wood" two versions, of "Scots Wha Hae" at least two, and so on throughout. Scott Douglas has rightly judged that the varied phases of the poet's mind are greatly matters of interest to his readers *and* students— for I discriminate — and he has with untiring diligence presented every known or hitherto unknown or accessible version, together with emendations and other corrections, all illustrated with such copious notes and verifications as leave absolutely nothing desirable or attainable. His is, and must long continue therefore to be, *the*

edition for the student, because, of Burns's " pock
o' sweeties," whether sweet *or nauseous*, we "hae
them a'" for Scott Douglas, to be gloated over—
and rolled like a sweet morsel under the tongue—
by the literary pathologist, curious in his quest
into Burns's internal moral economy; or to be
pecked at, and nibbled from, for booksellers' pot-
boiler *cabinet* editions. But in this unique edition
the general reader *must* submit to eat this *peck of
dirt* with his boll of corn. And yet, why need Scott
Douglas's publisher make this *compulsory?* There
can be few, if any, copies of the limited special
edition de luxe now attainable. The substantial
great cost has been already incurred, and is a
consideration of the past, while the very valuable
copyright remains unfructifying. It seems, therefore, that the enterprise which undertook and
carried through such a big job might with a light
heart enter on that of "a people's edition" of
Burns — a people's cabinet edition of Scott
Douglas's *edition de luxe*, for it merits that name.
Neither the repute of Burns nor that of this special
edition could suffer from such process as that
to which the Koh-i-noor was subjected. This
unequalled gem, when first presented to the Queen,

weighed above 184 carats, but its beauty and
even intrinsic value was blurred and defaced by
unsightly flaws, which, experts agreed, could, and
should, be removed.   This was done, and the
jewel, *reduced in its bulk* 'to a weight little
exceeding 122 carats, came out of the process
with a brilliancy and effect that has enhanced a
value that cannot well be estimated, and also has
rendered the gem absolutely unique.   There
would be little diminution in the colossal mass of
Burns through such very simple editing as would
be needful to pare down Scott Douglas's presentment.   And why should not the objectionable
excrescences be removed which mar its inherent
noble majesty?   Burns himself would, as it can be
shown, be the first to sanction the process, for in
reference to a precisely analogous condition of
things—the production of an edition of the poems
of Allan Ramsay — Burns wrote in April 1793
to Mr Thomson regarding certain alterations
made :

"I cannot approve of taking such liberties with an
author as Mr Walker has done. . . . Let the poet, if
he choose, take up the idea of another and work it into a
piece of his own, but to mangle the works of the poor
bard, whose tuneful tongue is now mute for ever in the

dark and narrow house, by Heaven 'twould be sacrilege! I grant that Mr Walker's version is an improvement, but I know Mr Walker well, and esteem him much; let him mend the song as a Highlander mended his gun; he gave it a new stock, a new lock, and a new barrel. *I do not by this object to taking out improper stanzas where that can be done without spoiling the whole.*"

And Burns goes on to point out such and such verses that *may be taken out with no bad results,* and others that *may be omitted with manifest improvement.* Now, this is really the entire case. There are a few poems of Burns, two or three, that may well be omitted entirely, and a few— say half-a-dozen—in which the omission of an occasional unprintable word or passage will *not* spoil the whole—would, indeed, never be missed except to the scent of some rabid first-edition Burnsite. On the contrary, it is their *presence* that *spoils the whole,* and bars the entrance of thousands into domains of literary delights. With the flow of time the impure sediment of Burns's writing will assuredly sink, and to other generations will be unknown, while the stream of true genius will go on for ever. This has been exemplified in Shakespeare. But why should the clarifying process be delayed? Again citing Burns himself on the side on which he would undoubtedly rank, as evidenced in his last interview with his greatly esteemed friend Mrs Riddell, to whom

> "*He lamented* that letters and verses *written with unguarded and improper freedom,* and which *he earnestly wished to have buried in oblivion,* would be handed about by *idle vanity or malevolence, when no dread of his resentment* would restrain them, or *prevent the censures of shrill-tongued malice,* or the insidious sarcasms of envy, from pouring forth *all their venom to blast his fame. He lamented* that he had written *many indifferent poetical pieces,* which *he feared* would now, with *all their imperfections on their head, be thrust upon the world.* On this account *he deeply regretted* having deferred to put his papers in a state of arrangement, as he was now (that is, a fortnight before his death) quite incapable of the exertion."

How clearly poor Burns at this trying hour foresaw some of the agencies which would "blast his fame," but he did not anticipate that the greatest injuries would proceed from his so-called friends. If any great man has had occasion to cry "Save me from my friends," it is Burns. In his latest, literally dying, hours there was

> "Not one immoral, one corrupted thought,
>   Not one impure sentence but he wished to blot."

And yet it is entirely his professed friends, who speak of "dear Rabbie" as of a brother, who studiously conserve all that he so condemned, repented, and lamented. I have quoted his latest wishes. It seems to me that he had another class in his mind likely to "blast his fame"—viz., those who "darkling grub this earthly hole, in low pursuit," and that to them he made the appeal and warning when, in his own epitaph, he wrote—

> " The poor inhabitant below
> Was quick to learn and wise to know,
> And keenly felt the friendly glow
>   And softer flame ;
> *But thoughtless follies* laid him low,
>   And stain'd his name."

It was his own father whom he so revered that he portrayed in the "Cottar's Saturday Night," as the head of the family circle, the "father, priest, and friend," who brings out the big Ha' Bible from which to read, and

> " *Wales* a portion wi' judicious care."

It should be easy for the publisher of the Scott Douglas edition to carry out the dying wishes of Burns, and in so doing place his memory

T

beyond reproach, and confer a boon upon the
greater mass of the reading public, which is
taught by men whom they cannot but respect,
that in touching Burns's writings, as served up
in most editions, they are touching pitch.   It
should be easy to obtain the services of an
editor—no great literary talent needed—who
would respect conventional usages and take
out the two or three throughout improper
poems, and the half-dozen or thereby improper
passages to be found in a few others, and do
this in disregard of pathological and convivial
students of Burns, unmindful of wail for "the
text, the whole text" of those "lovers of Burns,"
whose affection is much that of Tam o' Shanter
for Souter Johnnie.   There would be no need
to meddle with those poems which deal with
theological matters.   They may be judiciously
left undisturbed, as concerning subjects on which
opinion has long differed.   For Burns never
wrote to decry religion properly so-called.   He
tried to do away with *cant*, and to strip the
cloak of religion from off the shoulders of
the *hypocrite*.   Burns recognised that sensible
men and conscientious men all over the world

were of one religion. What a gain such an edition would be to the many who are, in the existing state of things, *compelled* to see what they would willingly *not perceive*. The " People's Complete Edition " which would result would unfailingly be that compromise effected between the burghers of Glasgow and the fanatic mob of the Reformation days when St Mungo's Cathedral, the prime jewel of our city, was threatened with utter destruction. But, as recorded by Andrew Fairservice, the opposing parties "Cam to an agreement to tak a' the idolatrous statues o' sants (sorrow be on them) out o' their neuks, and sae the *bits of stane idols* were broken in pieces by Scripture warrant, and flung into the Molendinar Burn, and the auld kirk stood as croose as a cat when the fleas are kaimed aff her, and a' body was alike pleased."

In parting with the fanatic Burnsite, my last words are to adjure him by what he may have in himself, becoming a pure-minded man, by such regard as he may have for the memory of a dead father, brother, or son, and by what respect he may have for himself *and for Burns*, to *honour Burns's last wishes.* (Appendix, Note L, p. 181.)

> " No farther seek his [*errors*] to disclose,
>   Or draw his *frailties* from their dread abode ;
> There they alike in trembling hope repose,
>   The bosom of his Father and his God."

There is much of wisdom and of morality in the saying : " He who falls into sin, is *a man;* if he repents, is *a saint;* and if he boasteth of it, is *a devil."*

I am very conscious that my detailed reminiscence of a long bygone time in a register of passing events has almost unconsciously been prolix, occupying space that many readers would prefer to see filled with the hourly stirring events of "a crisis of unparalleled significance in the world's history." But this consideration has weighed little with me, having seen so many of these unparalleled crises "blow over." *Tot homines, tot sententiis.* I have been writing for the gratification, I hope, of many readers, who, it may be, are little excited as to the punishment dealt to Panama Plunderers, and even indifferent whether the bellicose Ulster Colonel dies soon and peacefully in his bed, as I trust he may, or later in the last ditch of the distressful country, but who, as Scotsmen, are interested in aught that relates to personalities made conspicuous by the genius of Burns, and who, while Scotland stands where it did, will ever feel interested in Burns's Jean Armour, his Highland Mary and his Chloris, the Lassie wi' the Lintwhite Locks.

APPENDIX.

Note A.

" White Flower Love."

Page 110 of Text.

The phrase " white flower love," as applied to Burns, indicates those females of his acquaintance for whom he felt an admiration or regard that induced him to pay them poetical compliments, which he almost invariably did in the assumed character of a lover. And according to his brother Gilbert, he was in the habit of writing a song on almost every woman of his acquaintance, however slight the association. His " white flower loves " are therefore beyond estimate in number. But as illustrative of their character, I may cite Miss Alexander, "The Lass o' Ballochmyle"; Miss Davies, "Bonnie wee thing, cannie wee thing"; "Chloris"; Miss M'Murdo, "Bonnie Jean"; Jessie Lewars, "Here's a health to ane I lo'e dear."

By the "red flower loves" is indicated those females with whom Burns associated—held in pre-eminent fondness—and to whom he made proposals of marriage. Of

these I may cite Ellison Begbie, "On Cessnock Banks";
Mary Campbell, "Highland Mary"; Margaret Chalmers,
"My Peggy's Face"; Jean Armour, "The Poet's Wife";
Mrs M'Lehose, "Clarinda, mistress of my soul."

Towards such ladies as the refined and pious Mrs
Dunlop, and his "ever valued friend" Mrs Riddell, his
sentiments of admiration were those in which there was
no mixture of what is usually called love, but purely
the spiritual love or friendship of men and women
usually called "platonic."

Under none of these definitions is included the "Link
abrides" of Society—women of no reputation — with
whom "Love is liberty, and nature law."

Note B.

Imperfect Versions of Burns's Life and Writings.

Page 21 of Text.

I have already referred to several of the professedly
complete editions, no one of which satisfies the require-
ments of a *National,* or "People's Family Edition."
That of Robert Chambers, in my opinion, occupies the
foremost position, in its conception, and specially in its
character, being decorous in its language, conscientious
in execution, and fairly full in contents, *up to its date.*
But it has one objectionable element—a fault that,
although leaning to virtue's side, lays it open to adverse
criticism from all sides. This consists in its endeavour
to exclude the objectionable pieces, and portions of

pieces, which Burns so desired should be omitted.   But this commendable characteristic is the *crux* of the fanatic Burnsite contention ; and, he being *irreconcilable*, is a greater reason for his having no pretext.   And the fault in Chambers, for which no honest plea can be offered, is the introduction of poems not written by Burns, and the *amending* of others by *substituting* words or phrases as improvements on what is held to be otherwise not decently presentable.

There is thus a double cause for dissatisfaction to an earnest reader, who is uncertain what may have been kept in, or left out.   Scott Douglas, always truthful and accurate, does not fail to point to this act of heresy in Chambers.   In his comments on the poem "The Lass that made the Bed for Me," he says : "The song is much too warmly coloured to have found a place in Robert Chambers's edition, but he inserted *from a source he did not acknowledge*, a very innocent abridgment of it,* as pure as smiling infancy."   Cunningham had evidently been acquainted with the purified version, although he did not adopt it.   The author of the amended version was William Stenhouse, who supplied illustrative notes to *Johnson's Musical Museum* about the year 1820.

It was this same Mr Stenhouse who misled Chambers in his history of "the *fair* Rabina." In substituting Stenhouse's *reconstruction* of the "Lass that made the Bed," Chambers disregarded Burns's clearly expressed indication of what was permissible in dealing with a deceased poet's writings ; namely, *to leave out what is*

* More than an abridgment—a transformation.—J. A.

objectionable, and *not* "mend," except in the manner the Highlandman mended his gun. A *substitution* should be honestly labelled as a substitution, an amendment ticketed as an amendment, an omission indicated, and the reader should not be *hoodwinked*, even for his good. He may be seeking *the truth* when thus deceived. With this reference to *principles* involved, and with the rider that Chambers is not up to the present date in fulness of material now available, and requires revision in dates and facts, I greatly commend his work as the nearest approach we have of a model for general use. It must not be inferred that Chambers is *over rigidly* righteous in dealing with Burns's improprieties of language. The spirit in which he approaches the task of editor is thus expressed in his preface: "Burns's writings involve much that one cannot but think unhappily chosen in point of *subject* and *allusion;* but after all, who would wish even those which are most infelicitous in this respect, unwritten? I have not been rigorous in my selection of his writings—*a few passages excepted*—because I think there is a disposition in parties, and descendants of persons, whom certain of his poems once offended, to regard them as things having *now* only *a literary interest*, and to be judged of accordingly." In other passages he palliates the admission of words and phrases, not in consonance with modern notions of delicacy, and thinks they may be overlooked, as similar faults are tolerated in the writings of Sterne and other men of exceptional genius.

If Chambers's edition was revised, corrected in inaccuracies, and brought up to date in completeness

U

co-equal with that of Scott Douglas; or, if the edition of Scott Douglas was *purified* and made co-equal in that quality with Chambers's, there would in either case be a work assuredly meriting the confidence of 95 per cent. of *every class* of Burns's admirers.

To Scott Douglas's edition there applies the objection that he is an irreconcilable Burnsite, even more than the poet himself was, and he frankly admits that he is so, despite of Burns. He tells us that "Burns, when he felt himself dying, lamented his then physical disability and lost opportunities to *ensure* that none of his writings should go forth, *except such as should sustain* his *moral* and literary reputation—*feared the damage* to his good name *from the railings* of 'hackney scribblers';" and, continues Mr Douglas, "we may well wonder how so little regard has been paid to injunctions and wishes thus recorded, *both in the days of his strength and in the night of his woe.*" A dread of losing part of "that respect which man deserves from man" was a deeply-rooted feeling in Burns, as he records in a private journal which he kept locked. "The *world*, however," says Mr Douglas, "has decided, *in spite of the Bard's protestation, that every good, bad, and indifferent scrap* he is known to have penned shall be brought to light and examined." Instead of the "world," it would be more true to say that the decision is that of the jolly dogs and loose fishes of the world, pandered to by literary detectives and "hackney scribblers," who for prospective pay let themselves out to gratify ignoble cravings, indifferent to results on general society, or to the reputation of a man whom so many would gladly honour for the good he *has* done, and *could still* do, and who atoned in his bitter repentance for the evil he had done.

I respect much in Scott Douglas, and sorrowfully realise that he, by analogy, illustrates in the moral world a condition frequent in the physical, *i.e.*, that of individuals who are "colour-blind"—cannot distinguish red from green or black. Mr Douglas seems incapable of recognising improprieties in language—at least of appraising their importance, at least their unconventionality—even as Allan Cunningham is, in the capacity, *or disposition*, to keep truth apart from unscrupulous and motiveless fiction. I have a theory on this point that I will bring forward in a special note. Mr Douglas so far concedes to conventional decency, that of a blackguard ballad, revised by Burns for *Johnson's Museum*, called "Had I the Wyte," and which Douglas admits is "*bordering* on indelicacy," he says, "it is purity itself beside the old model that suggested it." Indeed, Scott Douglas, in his indifference on such matters, reminds me of the chorus of a doggerel street ballad, "But, it's aal one, it's aal one, it's aal one, to Tonal."

Passing from Scott Douglas to Allan Cunningham is a transition from light to darkness, for the former, despite his one badly apologised-for fault, is as invariably honest, truthful, and scrupulously conscientious, as the latter is unscrupulous and unreliable. A clever and versatile writer, he utilised his luxuriant imagination in *inventing* facts and anecdotes *de omnibus rebus*, and his piquant annotations gave a zest to the fine pictured illustrated edition that he was entrusted to edit. His presentment of Burns, his life and writings, therefore had for some time considerable popularity, which it may still have among the indifferent or badly informed. But it soon transpired that he had acted unfairly by Burns and his writings, for, so early as in the 1834 edition, he apologised (under publicity of convictions) for having inserted *writings of others* among those of Burns: *ex gratia* the poem of "On Evan Banks" by Miss Williams, the song of "Shelah O'Neal" by Sir Alexander Boswell. He made very lame and far from satisfactory explanations of how he had fallen into "error," and asked continuance of confidence by an assurance that in *this* edition "I have omitted no piece of either prose or verse, which bore the impress of his hand, *nor included any* by which his reputation would likely be impaired." But beyond acknowledgment of convicted mis-statements, he continued his progress in "the worser way." The first poem I examined to test his accuracy, or *disposition* to be accurate, was the song "Of a' the airts the wind can blaw," written by Burns in 1786, soon after his marriage, and while living alone at Ellisland, getting his farm-house in order to receive his wife. This song consists of four verses of four lines each, and Burns *made no after additions to it.* But the song became popular, and additions were made *by others*, among whom is Mr John Hamilton, a respectable music-seller in Edinburgh. He, after Burns's death, wrote four additional stanzas, possessing considerable merit.* But Mr Hamilton composed

* His addition begins "O blaw, ye wastlin winds blaw saft."

under the erroneous notion that the absence of Jean was that of the period *before marriage*, when she removed to Paisley to avoid Burns. Under this mistake, Hamilton makes the poet implore the "wastlin winds" to "bring the lassie back" to him, when he had only to *return to her*, and who, moreover, could not come "back" to Ellisland, *where she had never been*. These facts, with certain differences in the rhythm of the added verses, were sufficient to distinguish the apocryphal additions, and have been critically commented on by various writers—among others by Hately Waddell—although such labour has long been needless, because of the facts being sufficiently notorious. But Cunningham, in his account of the song, boldly says "other versions are abroad, *this one is from the manuscript of the poet*," and he straightway gives Hamilton's four verses, consisting of sixteen lines, *in continuation* of Burns's sixteen lines.

There is usually motive for crime, even the sin of untruth, as in more serious crimes. That prince among liars, the "fat knight" of Shakespeare, when he invented the fifty men in buckram suits, whose united onslaught he withstood unaided, at his rapier's point (carefully hacked with his dagger, *ecce signum*), had for his motive to establish a reputation for bravery, and to avoid the imputation of cowardice. But what motive can be imagined as influencing Cunningham? And in parallel illustration, what motive could he have for vilifying the reputation of various individuals who had never crossed his path, and could not? what motive, for example, for fixing a calumny on the repute of Johnson, a sincere and much regarded friend of Burns, who did much to show his regard for Johnson?

Burns, on 17th June 1796, and when on his death-bed, wrote to Johnson, requesting a copy of Johnson's *Scots Musical Museum*, in four volumes, to which he had been so voluminous a contributor. Burns asked it, that he might present it to Jessie Lewars, who was then nursing him, and he begged it by return, for he felt time was setting with him. Johnson *instantly responded*, and sent the volumes, *by return*, so speedily, indeed, that on 26th June, Burns wrote on the fly-leaf of the first volume, a poem in twelve lines, addressed to Miss Lewars, expressive of the dying man's gratitude to his kind friend and nurse.

The poem, which will be found in many editions of Burns, begins

> " Thine be the volumes, Jessy fair,
>   And with them, take the poet's prayer ; "

and the poem concludes,

> " These be thy guardian and reward,
>   So prays thy faithful friend the Bard."

The volume with the inscription was exhibited at Dumfries on the occasion of the Burns Centenary in 1859.

Notwithstanding the notoriety of these facts, we find Cunningham, who could know nothing personally of the circumstances, writing some forty years after their occurrence, even in his latest edition, "will it be believed that this humble request was not complied with!" And the calumny he repeats in a note to a letter of Burns, thus:—"Few of the last requests of the poet were effectual: Clarke, *it is believed*, did not send the second pound note he wrote for; *Johnson did not send the copy of the Museum which he requested*, and the Commissioners of Excise refused the continuance of his full salary."

In the Edinburgh subscription list, set afloat immediately after Burns's death, there appears the name of Johnson, for four pounds, and he was a poor man, an engraver in a small way, and subsisting by his hand labour. Now, what possible motive could Cunningham have for this malignant vilification of poor Johnson, or of various others whom he unsparingly traduced—*after their death!* To Burns himself he did not act with the loyalty becoming a biographer and a professing admirer. With the skill, and seemingly the chuckling glee of a Mephistopheles, he made openings, through which he might drag forth, burnish, and show in bright relief, the lower qualities of Burns, real or imputed. He urged that if Burns failed as a farmer, it was his own fault—that he had no real knowledge, only lip knowledge, of farming—no real love for it—no heart in it; while professedly engaged at husbandry, he was dreaming of, and in pursuit of, sweethearts—preferred attendance at drinking meetings, and so on. Cunningham so far speaks truth as to the neglect that attended some of Burns's last requests, in particular, it may be noted, that his writings of an objectionable kind might not be "raked up by hackney scribblers" to his discredit. *This request* Cunningham *disregarded*, and by his attractive notes, and figments of the brain, kept scandals alive and created a mine from which inferior scribblers, and speculative booksellers, have since drawn largely. At this moment I have before me a handsomely got up little cabinet volume of Burns (E. Moxon & Co., publishers; Rossetti, editor), in which I find, within three pages, two of the apocryphal poems "Evan Banks" and "Shelah O'Neal," for the discovery and insertion of which Cunningham was called to account above sixty years ago. In other small editions I occasionally find his untruthful annotations reproduced. So true it is that the evil that men do lives after them. What conjecture can reach the period, when the mischievous effects of Cunningham's luxuriant "efforts of fancy" will die out?

I find in a memorandum some notes I have made on other two editions of Burns, and to these I make passing mention, chiefly because they bear on their title pages the attractive lure of the names of two clergymen, viz., that of Rev. George Gilfillan and P. Hately Waddell, *Minister of the Gospel.* The first bears the title of "The *Poetical* Works of Robert Burns, with *Memoir, Critical Dissertation,* and *Explanatory Notes*" (Edinburgh, 1856; Nichol, publisher). Of its alleged contents, I note that the poems consist of 232 in all, given without dates, chronological, or other arrangement, but huddled promiscuously; miscellaneous lengthy pieces, followed and

mixed up with songs, versicles, and such spurious pieces
as those for which Cunningham had to make apology.
The objectionable poems of Burns are included. The
scanty memoir, and critical dissertation, are obviously the
only contributions of Mr Gilfillan to this poor pot-boiler
edition, for of *editorial supervision* there is no evidence.
The meagre footnotes are the work of some one, who
veils himself under the initial B., and are of a quality that
might be supplied by any printer's devil of two years'
apprenticeship. The memoir and critique are comprised
in about forty pages of fierce, scathing *denunciation and
declamation* of the kind characteristic of Gilfillan, not
only on platforms but at the usually privileged friendly
dinner table,—no doubt familiar to those who have
associated with him,—aptly conveyed in the words, "I
am Sir Oracle, and when I ope my mouth, let no dog
bark." In fulminating his judgments, he tells us that
Burns was a man of inconsistencies, everything by turns
and nothing long, yielding to all impulses, good or bad
—high or low—the spirit of many of his songs—intensely
and grossly sensual; and Mr Gilfillan has ensured that
the worst specimens will be found in the work to which
he contributes his name as responsible for the compila-
tion. Burns is in his conception a compost of dirt and
deity—filth and fire—a living mirror that reflects in-
differently the dunghill at his door, or the evening star,
but with more pleasure the former. His coarseness, his
tinkler's jaw, smells of the smithy, and you hear the
clatter of the gill-stoup. He has nothing to say in
extenuation of poor Burns's frailties—nothing of the

X

forbearing, long-suffering, charitable consideration that he, Gilfillan himself, exacted, required, and received so much of from those perforce associating with him, as also from the general public, and which they rendered because of the *intrinsic good qualities* he was known to possess.   Admirers of Burns will find little to give pleasure, or satisfy judgment, in Gilfillan's scathing critique, and much to give dissatisfaction, tempered, however, by the knowledge that the laboured effort of vituperative censure was, as I have heard one of his best friends say, "only pretty Fanny's way."   No reader need look for materials on which to base a just estimate of Burns and his work, from the pages of the Rev. George Gilfillan.

There remain among my notes, references to the portly quarto volume, outwardly resembling the traditionary " big Ha' Bible," that bears to comprise " The Life and Works of Robert Burns," by P. Hately Waddell, *Minister of the Gospel* (Glasgow, 1867; Wilson, publisher).   It will, from the catching designation on its forefront, be naturally assumed that the manly, dignified protest of the Rev. Norman Macleod, so becoming a " Minister of the Gospel," would find an able backer in Mr Waddell, himself a man of known literary talent.   His work consists of a higgledy-piggledy agglomeration of various early editions and collections, chiefly published in Burns's lifetime—a huge " cantle " from Currie's editions, and voluminous criticisms and commentaries of Mr Waddell himself.   So far from joining forces with his two brother " Ministers of the Gospel," Mr Waddell has· little or nothing to say in the way of censure. But he is a dangerous commentator nevertheless, for he has plenty to say in extenuation or approval of what Burns himself was ashamed and grieved over; but this by the way. Mr Waddell's edition is a strange specimen of book-making, having neither alphabetical nor chronological arrangement, built up of divisions and yet again divisions, of additions and still addenda, but substantially consisting of reproductions of Currie, and other imperfect issues, comprising the early Kilmarnock publications, much commentary, conjectures, erroneous statements, and very incomplete withal. Pleading for what Burns did not extenuate, Mr Waddell says of one objectionable poem (found in all the editions I have named excepting that of Chambers), he says that "it is a revision of a licentious old song to render it capable of admission into the *Museum* (Johnson's). In this revision he has removed, *as far as possible*, the actual licence, and has otherwise *atoned for improprieties* by the *infusion of natural pathos*. In his hands, in short, it contains on a painful and disgraceful topic, *a defence or exculpation of sin or error* by a narrative of facts, not worse than we see recorded and minutely detailed every day in the public proceedings of the Divorce Court. *More need not be said* on such a topic." Regarding other poems of a like kind, Mr Waddell says, "Nor is there, in the *morality* of these popular lyrics, of which he had more reason to be ashamed than in that of others which he never hesitated to avow."

Such are a sample of Mr Waddell's comments on songs taken from *Johnson's Museum, not acknowledged by Burns,* some of which he *admittedly annotated or recast;* but, as Mr Waddell admits, *very few, if any, of which* he was spared ever *to acknowledge publicly. Johnson's Museum* contains 222 pieces, of which Burns acknowledges 108. Regarding the remainder, whether revised or in fragments, consisting of 114 pieces, no *acknowledgment or claim* was ever made by Burns. But he had been touching pitch, and he was defiled. For, as he was *a genius,* all the pitch that bore the mark of *talent* has been placed to his account. And regarding such productions, "*more,*" says Mr Waddell, "Minister of the Gospel," *need not be said.* After such a statement from a minister of the gospel—

> " Religion blushing, veils her sacred fires,
> And unawares, morality expires."

NOTE C.

ALLAN CUNNINGHAM'S UNVERACITY.

Page 31 of Text.

The frequency, quantity, and quality of Allan Cunningham's misrepresentations have caused me to reflect seriously, from a medical point of view, as to his being mentally responsible for the habitual disregard of truth I have reprobated, and of which I have given sufficient illustration. He was a man of considerable talent, *cela va sans dire,* and "great wits to madness nearly are allied." There are young children who will look in your face and tell you, without winking, the most improbable and impossible stuff—"airy nothings"—and there are cases of mild lunacy characterised by the like peculiarity. The distinction between fact and fiction seems to them as impracticable as is the distinction between red, blue, or black to a man who is colour-blind. With even the soundest intellect, the transition from thought to thought is unconsciously automatic—cause and effect alternate. The homicidal lunatic hears a voice *we* cannot hear prompting a sudden bloody impulse. He reasons, but on wrong premises, and follows out what seems the legitimate conclusion. The railway conductor or ship-watch sees what he takes to be the red signal of danger, and his consequent action brings disastrous collision. In these cases, where there is a defect in the perceptive faculties, the erroneous perception is a motive, and although Cunningham's unscrupulous disregard of fact seems to have been motiveless, the voice we cannot hear may to him have been as real as the "dagger of the mind" which to Macbeth was "as palpable as that he clutched," while irresistibly marshalled on the path to crime. How are we to get at Cunningham's initial motive and false deductions? Let us consider his baseless statement that Chloris's husband, "a southron," was an English officer of the army. Chloris had been wooed by two suitors, one a Mr Gillespie, often alluded to as "an officer of the Excise." He was, in truth, fellow-official with Burns. The other was Mr Whelpdale, the young, showy, spendthrift farmer from Cumberland, who settled on the farm of Barnhill, adjoining Chloris's father's residence. Chloris did not marry the "officer," but

married the showy "southron." Cunningham got
mixed, and retained the ideas of a marriage, a showy
Englishman, and an officer, and being quick at con-
clusions, luxuriantly imaginative and unscrupulous, he
instantly jotted down a coherent illustrative annotation.
His process of reasoning must have been of that kind
pursued by Captain Fluellen, when he proved to his own
satisfaction that the countries of Greece and of Wales
were one and the same. "If you look on the maps of
the world, I warrant you shall find in the comparisons
between Macedon and Monmouth, that the situations,
look you, is both alike. There is a river in Macedon;
and there is also, moreover, a river at Monmouth; it is
called Wye, at Monmouth; but it is out of my brains
what is the name of the other river; but 'tis all one, 'tis
alike as my fingers is to my fingers, and there is salmons
in both." In some such fashion Cunningham may, by a
swift process of intuition, have jumped at his conclusion
that Chloris's husband was "an English officer of the
army," for in the Excise as in the Army there is "*officers
in both.*" If this is the explanation, then our "pity, perhaps our charity," should incline us to regret much of
the censure that Allan Cunningham is liable to.

But the strain on our charity will be great, when we
are considering the following, among so many similar
illustrations. Scott Douglas, vol. v. p. 457, tells us that
not less than twenty-two "spurious notes" *professing to
be written by Burns,* and appended to songs published
by Cromek in 1808 and 1810, are "the deliberate manu-
facture of Allan Cunningham."

Note D.

Burns's National Songs.

Page 56 of Text.

The song, " She says she loe's me best of a'," may be cited among many to illustrate the pre-eminent genius of Burns as a writer of songs, *characteristic of nationality.* Tom Moore has often been called the "Burns of Ireland." But, although a true poet—not a mere versifier—and universally admired, he is not a *national* poet in the sense that Burns is. It chances that both poets wrote songs to the same air, " Oonagh's Waterfall,"— genuine Irish, by the way, and so far in favour of Moore's performance. The first verse of his song goes thus:

> " While gazing on the moon's light,
>   A moment from her smile I turned,
> To look at orbs that more bright,
>   In lone and distant glory burned.
> But too far, each proud star,
>   For me to feel its kindling flame ;
> Much more dear, that mild sphere,
>   That near our planet smiling came.
> Thus Mary be thou, but my own,
>   While brighter eyes unheeded play,
> I'll love those moonlight looks alone,
>   Which bless my home, and guide my way."

Here it is at once evident that the lyric suits a Scotsman, Irishman, or Persian equally well—that the versification is polished, smooth, and flowing, the rhyme perfect, and the sentiment pleasing, but that one or more

stanzas are needed to complete a single image. The
contrast with Burns's song is great.   For in it the rhyme
is not equal to Moore's, but there is sentiment and
human sympathy evoked by the first line, and *national
sentiment with national scenery* are equally evolved in
the last verse, where the lines " By wimpling burn and
leafy shaw " appeal so dearly and quickly to a Scotsman's
sentiments.   Completed images are conveyed in a couple
of words, while image follows image, and phrase follows
phrase, in happy appropriateness, until, as from stroke
upon stroke of a hammer, sentiments are linked in
harmonious association as melody is assured in the
recurring rhythm of a waltz.

> " Sae warming, sae charming,
>   Her faultless form, and gracefu' air,"

realises before the mind's eye the object of admiration,
and the

> " Dewy eve, and rising moon,
>   Fair beaming, and streaming,
>   Her silver light the boughs amang,"

conjure up the local surroundings with pleasing emotions.
If the two songs are read in continuation by any one
who knows the melody, he will find it difficult afterwards
to dissociate the words of Burns, or to associate the
words of Moore, with the melody.   In "Their Groves
of Green Myrtle" how swiftly a Scotsman is, in fancy,
wafted to scenes of early days,—to "Yon lone glen of
green *brecken*, wi' the *burn* stealing under the *lang yellow
Broom;*" and searches again where "the *Blue Bell*

and *Gowan* lurk lowly unseen "—and despite "*Cauld Caledonia's blast*" wanders "as free as the winds of his *Mountains*" hand in hand with *his* Jean.

As a national poet, Burns stands easily *facile princeps*, and there "isna ane to peer him."

NOTE E.

"O, THAT'S THE LASSIE O' MY HEART."

Page 97 of Text.

"Will any one," says Hately Waddell, "produce now, from any European language, dead or living, a parallel in taste, in elegance, in delicacy, and in perfection of composition, to 'Wha is she that lo'es me.'" Mr Waddell gives the first line of the text erroneously, but I do not so confidently take up his challenge on the merits of the song. I comment on the song for another object. The air "Morag," or "The Young Highland Drover," to which the lyric is set, was a very special favourite with Burns. It is a genuine Highland air, and by many considered beautiful. It is plaintive and complicated; but the rhythm of each stanza is halting, and conveys the idea of lameness, from the use of a fifth line. Indeed, it is somewhat strange that Burns, who was so "stumped" by "the peculiarity" of rhythm in the air "Caledonian Hunt's Delight" (see song No. 26), that he found it impossible to make a second stanza to suit, was nevertheless able to furnish the delightful

Y

song that evokes Mr Waddell's enthusiastic panegyric.
But there was in Burns this peculiarity, that although
not possessing what is usually considered a quick ear for
melody, and having poor capacity as a vocalist, he nevertheless had a keen perception of notes as he heard
them sung or played over.   They seemed to strike
responsive chords which awoke melody in his heart,
and prompted emotions and sentiments, which he linked
with the air.   I knew an individual whose gift in this
respect often occasioned me much surprised speculation.
For being myself passionately fond of music, and having
had a quick appreciative ear, and dabbling in all kinds of
instruments available for solo performers, I have often
endured long martyrdoms while this gentleman paced
up and down an apartment with Irish bagpipes strapped
under his arm, occasionally illustrating with his rasping
voice, which had a compass decently extending through
say five notes, but which all unconsciously to its owner
now wandered promiscuous from major to minor key,
from grave to falsetto, from lively to severe accidental
sharps or flats.   And yet he could criticise correctly, and
with an appreciation that a professional artist might be
proud of, such performances of public performers as we
at times enjoyed in each other's companionship.   The
melody and the harmony were locked up in his inner
man, and in his inward consciousness there was the key.
So it was with Burns, for after, with patient attention and
effort, he picked up an air, no consciousness of his
personal disability restrained him from a frank expression
of his appreciation of faults of rhythm or of accentua-

tion, and boldly holding his ground in opposition to pretentious virtuosos such as Thomson, who, with a ludicrously painful incapacity in judging the special suitability of particular airs to particular songs, often lectured Burns, who, however, turned occasionally on his mentor and gave him a lesson with all the gravity of one who was conscious of speaking within his capacity. Such a lecture, amusing when we consider to whom it was addressed, and instructive as illustrating the melody within his soul of which Burns was so conscious, will be found in a letter he sent to Thomson, October 19, 1794. It is too long for quotation, but I may give a portion. He says, *inter alia*, " In the meantime, let me offer as a new improvement, or rather *a restoring of old simplicity*, in one of your newly adopted songs :

> ' When she cam ben she bobbit, (a crotchet stop)
>   When she cam ben she bobbit ; (a crotchet stop)
> And when she cam ben, she kiss'd Cockpen,
>   And syne denied that she did it.' (a crotchet stop)

This is the old rhythm, and by far the most original and beautiful. Let the harmony of the bass at the stops be full, and thin and dropping through the rest of the air, and you will give the tune a noble and striking effect," etc.

The air and the words of "O wat ye wha that lo'es me" are admirably suited in conjunction, and if sung *con amore, con spirito,* by a likely young fellow not afraid to let out his voice, or to let in to his countenance a little expression differing from that of a hairdresser's model or of a conventional stage tenor, he will assuredly score a success. It grates upon me to see a young man

with a little hair on his upper lip, and of inches to make
a man, stand up in a drawing-room and "wawl," in the
plaintive tone and accents of a sick girl, that his "Nannie's
awa" or that he'll "lay doon his heid an' dee." There
is in these occasional performances such incongruity in
the long-drawn-out, mellifluous cadences, and the actuality
that an animated being is—to his conception—realising
human emotion, that I unavoidably recall Hamlet's sensa-
tions under somewhat analogous conditions, where he
says, "Oh, it offends me to the soul, to hear a robustious
periwig-pated fellow tear a passion to tatters, to very
rags," etc. In the converse it is loathsome to witness a
young fellow wanting the pluck to

" Stand up, and speak up, and make her be sensible,
How she's in luck, that can get such a fencible."

O, wat ye wha that lo'es me, And has my heart a keep-ing? O,
sweet is she that lo'es me, As dews o' sum-mer weep-ing, In
Chorus.
tears the rose-buds steep-ing! O, that's the las-sie o' my heart, My
las-sie ev-er dear-er, O, she's the queen o' woman-kind, And
ne'er a ane to peer her.

The air "Morag" is not very accessible, and I cannot doubt that in supplying a score of the notes, I am likely to gratify some, alike for the melody as for interest in an air that was a great favourite of Burns.

NOTE F.

"THE FAIR RABINA."

Page 110 *of Text.*

"O turn again, thou fair Rabina." That Cunningham knew anything of the identity of "a real lady, and a lovely one," real or imputed, bearing this unusual name, is improbable. An annotator, more scrupulous and with better opportunities than he, viz., Mr Stenhouse, has failed. Cunningham took up his quest, if he made any quest, many years later, and he so rarely had any *actual* basis for *his* statements that were not matters of notoriety, that it is inconceivable he did possess any item of fact without making pointed reference to the clue. His *facts* were too rare not to be made the most of. The true history is conclusively established by Scott Douglas, and we are left to conjecture. I think it probable that Johnson's text in three words, "the fair Rabina," was a jocular trap set to test if Burns's poetical powers were really equal to his boast, that he required only a hint, tall or short, fair or black, and he would furnish a poem. Upon that hint I conjecture that Johnson spake, and as Burns's pet cognomen among his admirers was "Rab"—

continues indeed to be Rab, the name Rabina as a feminine derivative was coined for the nonce. Burns had fallen into the trap, and came triumphantly through his self-imposed task, never dreaming that Johnson's "fair Rabina" was other than an honest flesh and blood damsel such as he was accustomed to deal with. He frankly admits that in Johnson's bald text he had his work cut out for him, but he got through it, and possibly with as little labour as an auld licht minister could, from such an exciting text as "the scorner's chair," or "fight the good fight," evolve a full-fledged theological discourse under sixteen or seventeen heads, and occupying an entire forenoon, afternoon, and evening of church service.

NOTE G.

"THE SONG OF DEATH."

Page 115 *of Text.*

There is in the Burns Museum at Kilmarnock, a copy of this poem in the handwriting of Thomas Campbell, the poet, author of the "Pleasures of Hope," and other standard classical lyrics of British literature. The history of this document is interesting, and illustrates the admiration in which Burns was held by a contemporary poet little more than twenty years younger than himself. Campbell was one at a festive gathering in the Albemarle Hotel, London, in 1836, at which Templeton, the vocalist, was also present, and was asked by Campbell to sing "The Song of Death." Templeton was doubtful of the words, whereupon Campbell procured pen, ink, and paper, and wrote the song from memory. Templeton then sang with an effect of the happiest kind, Campbell in particular being enthusiastically delighted, declaring that, often as he had heard it sang, he had never heard it so nobly rendered as by Templeton, whom he regarded as the foremost vocalist of the day. He added that this was the finest song Burns had written, and sufficient to have immortalised him if he had never written another. He remarked that it was a happy coincidence that Burns and Templeton were both Ayrshire men, and he wrote at the bottom of the copy, "To John Templeton, Esq., in memory of his singing this song." The song thus copied from memory contains several variations in the words, not to be found in Burns, a circumstance natural enough. The incident is chiefly interesting as a record of the opinion of a high art critic—himself a poet—and strongly imbued with the patriotic and chivalric fervour to which he gives expression in "Ye Mariners of England," "Battle of the Nile," of "Hohenlinden," and other patriotic outbursts. Templeton, of whose singing I have a vivid recollection, while *not* the foremost vocalist of his day, was for some time neck and neck with Sims Reeves in public favour as an opera singer, at a time when John Wilson, *the* singer *par excellence* of Scottish songs, was somewhat declining in power. I have heard the three, frequently, on the stage of the Edinburgh Theatre Royal and elsewhere; witnessed the effects they produced on large audiences; and listened to the discussions of able music critics on their respective merits. Thus, in opera, the singing of "Still so gently o'er me stealing," in "La Somnambula," by Templeton was considered unapproachable; that of Reeves in the last scene of "Lucia di Lammermoor" not anywhere surpassed. In the singing of *Scottish* songs, the test was a severe one before judges who had heard Wilson. Reeves judiciously restricted himself in the rendering of Scottish songs, although I have heard great applause follow his performance of "My love is like a red, red rose," but nothing approaching to the effects following on Templeton's stock song of "There lives a young lassie far doun in yon glen," which he rendered with a *verve* of passion that raised an audience to manifestations of highest gratified feeling. But, oh! the difference between them and Wilson,—the former almost invariably the presentments of the conventional, professional tenor, from whom one cannot dissociate a large, white shirt front, and a sheet of music held in the white-gloved hand, and from whose countenance human expression is excluded. But Wilson was a man, not a singing machine, really an animated being. To hear him, as he held immense audiences enthralled, and unconscious of shame—for the tears in their eyes became universal in their neighbours'—and in the abandon of uncontrollable mirth, was a life-remembered joy. "The Flowers of the Forest," "Go fetch to me a pint o' wine," "Muirland Willie," etc., etc., occur to me as illustrations. In the first, the pathetic reproach of "Oh, fickle fortune, why this cruel sporting," the despairing defiance of

"Thy frowns canna fear me, thy smiles canna cheer me."
In the "pint o' wine," the wrapt attitude, straining eyes
which seemed to see the "glittering spears" which were
"rankèd ready," but which were not the cause of grief;
only the "leaving thee, my bonie Mary." And in
"Muirland Willie" he would set young and old actually
shrieking with merriment and frantic applause, as with
a blue bonnet on his head he sang and enacted the lads
and lasses at Willie's marriage, "an aye they bobbit and
aye they becked, and cleeked, and crossed, and merrily
set, with a fal de ral lal," etc., etc. He literally, and with
contagious *abandon*, "merrily ranted and sang," snapping
and cracking his fingers, capering all the while across
the stage, affecting to kiss the bride he had secured in
bluff, brief wooing, making his "bannet" go spinning
into the side scenes, and winding up in a rhapsody of
song and merriment at the climax. There was in
Wilson's rendering of Scottish songs the hitherto un-
approached combination of a perfect actor, an eloquent
orator, and a vocalist possessing the sweetest, most
finely modulated, powerful, and, in its perfect harmony,
far reaching voice, conjoined with a *timbre*, that instantly
suggested the emotion of the singer,—a combination
altogether of qualities that, to my experience, and I
have, I think, heard all the eminent vocalists that have
been heard in this country during the past sixty or
seventy years,—surpasses all who have trod the stage
or orchestra platform. While Wilson was available, all
Scottish eyes and ears were idly turned on whoever
might follow him in his special domain of song.

Z

NOTE H.

"POT BOILER."

Page 120 of Text.

This slang phrase is employed in the studios of painters, sculptors, and literary artists to indicate work kept in stock or on hand to be disposed of, for immediate cash payment, to keep the domestic pot boiling.   The painter who has a number of landscapes, or of copies of the Old Masters, to meet the demand of "the picture dealer," calls his goods "pot boilers"—the French artist terms his goods "faire du metier," that is, "for the trade."   And artists of all denominations, discriminate work kept for *ready disposal,* from that which is executed for *love of the subject*—executed with a view to future fame, glory, or reputation, irrespective of immediate pecuniary recompense.   Printers, publishers, and booksellers, who vamp up speculative issues of old or unlikely stock, with *new title pages and prefaces,* or append some literary name, as *nominal editor,* have their goods designated throughout the trade as "pot-boiler editions."   And of these *there are gradations,* in the lower depths of which are to be found those publishers indicated by Robert Chambers, "who would sacrifice the highest interests of humanity to put an additional penny into their own purses," and to the lasting grief of all friends of our poet, "allowed the honour of the press" to those *unrevised* writings, the *unguarded and improper freedom* of which Burns lamented and "*earnestly wished to have buried in oblivion.*"

NOTE J.

MRS BURNS ON CHLORIS.

Page 124 of Text.

Hately Waddell informs us that Jean Armour, the poet's wife, had a warm regard for Jean Lorimer, and would not hear an ill word said of her. To Mr M'Diarmid, Mrs Burns said, "Jean Lorimer was the daughter of William Lorimer, Farmer, of Kemmis Hall, and in good circumstances. He had two daughters and three sons. His wife was given to drinking, and that injured his daughters. Jean used to visit at Ellisland. She had remarkably fair hair, and was perfectly virtuous. She took the fancy of an Englishman at a Moffat ball, and was married to him at Gretna Green. The man was a reprobate, but his mother allowed her an annuity." Such is Mrs Burns's succinct, round, unvarnished summary of Chloris's history, and intimacy with herself and her husband.

NOTE K.

OATHS.

Page 130 of Text.

Burns never approached in coarseness, extravagance, or irreverence, more especially in the use of sacred names, the language so prevalent among the upper classes of his own, or of subsequent time. The hard swearing, consisting of strings of inconsequential;

nonrelative coarse and violent "damns," etc., made no part of Burns's oaths, which consisted rather of vehement passionate adjurations of the nature of the favourite oath of another great man, William the Conqueror, who was in the habit of swearing "By the Splendour of God!" Burns, to give emphasis to earnest emotion, would swear "By the Celestial Powers," "By yon Starry Roof," "By a' that's guid," "By Heaven and Earth," and rarely employed—save in quotation—strong "Theological Language." But he held that "divines may say of what they please; I maintain that a hearty blast of execration is to the mind, what breaking a vein is to the body; the overloaded sluices of both are wonderfully relieved by their respective evacuations."

In forming a judgment on the moral tendency and taste of an author's writings of an epoch differing from our own, it would be as unfair to test them by the standard of the present day, as it would be to judge the dress of our ancestors by the fashions of the present day. What we now regard as offences against decorum and decency, might be shown to be the habit of the court of Queen Elizabeth. Civilised corruption and sensuality must be discriminated from simplicity and rustic barbarism. The man of society, who eats peas from a plate with the use of a fork, at one period helped himself with his fingers to mutton cutlets, from a trencher common to his neighbours; and in the revolving customs of an age, the time will come when our descendants will read almost with disbelief that there were in the present day scores of mothers who took their daughters to see "Frou Frou," or Adrienne Lecouvreur, and that neither mother nor daughter shrank with horror at situations analogous being discussed at Society's tea tables.

NOTE L.

REMONSTRANCE WITH BURNS BIOGRAPHERS.

Page 148 of Text.

It has chanced, strangely enough, that while passing these sheets through the press, I have seen a poem by Charles Mackay, LL.D., which so happily expresses the sentiments that I think are becoming all who profess admiration or respect for our national poet, that I am tempted to give it in full.

AT THE GRAVE OF ROBERT BURNS.

A *Remonstrance* with some of his Biographers.

CHARLES MACKAY, LL.D.

> Let him rest, let him rest ;
> The green earth on his breast ;
> And leave, oh ! leave his fame, unsullied by your breath.
> Each day that passes by,
> What meaner mortals die,
> What thousand raindrops fall into the sea of death
>
> No vendor of a tale
> (His merchandise for sale)
> Pries into evidence to show how *mean* were they.
> No *libel* touches *them ;*
> No *curious fools* condemn ;
> Their *human frailties* sleep for God, not man, to weigh.

And shall the Bard alone,
Have all his *follies* known,
Dug from the past, to spice a needless book—
That envy may exclaim
At mention of his name—
The *greatest are but small*, however great they look !

Let them rest, their sorrows o'er,
All the mighty bards of yore ;
Or if, ye *grubbers up of scandals dead and gone*,
To find amid the slime
Some sin of ancient time,
Some fault, or seeming fault, that Shakespeare might have done.

Some spot on Milton's truth,
Or Byron's glowing youth,
Some error not too small for miscroscopic gaze—
Shroud it in deepest gloom
As on *your father's* tomb
You'd hush the evil tongues that spoke in *his* dispraise ;

Shroud it in deepest night,
Or if *compelled to write*,
Tell us the inspiring tale of *perils* overcome,
Of *struggles for the good*,
Of *courage unsubdued*,
But let their *frailties* rest, or—on their faults *be dumb*.

INDEX.

2 A

Printed by M'FARLANE & ERSKINE, *Edinburgh.*

www.ingramcontent.com/pod-product-compliance
Lightning Source LLC
Chambersburg PA
CBHW022352020726
47500CB00002B/241